WILDCATS OF TONTO BASIN

Center Point
Large Print

Also by Nelson C. Nye and available from Center Point Large Print:

Wide Loop
The Killer of Cibecue

WILDCATS OF TONTO BASIN

NELSON C. NYE

CENTER POINT LARGE PRINT
THORNDIKE, MAINE

Originally published in the US by Phoenix Press.
Originally published in the UK by Wight and Brown.

The text of this Large Print edition is unabridged.
In other aspects, this book may vary
from the original edition.
Printed in the United States of America
on permanent paper.
Set in 16-point Times New Roman type.

ISBN: 978-1-64358-270-2 (hardcover)
ISBN: 978-1-64358-274-0 (paperback)

Library of Congress Cataloging-in-Publication Data

Names: Nye, Nelson C. (Nelson Coral), 1907-1997, author.
Title: Wildcats of Tonto Basin / Nelson C. Nye.
Description: Center Point Large Print edition. | Thorndike, Maine :
    Center Point Large Print, 2019.
Identifiers: LCCN 2019017040| ISBN 9781643582702 (hardcover :
    alk. paper) | ISBN 9781643582740 (paperback : alk. paper)
Subjects: LCSH: Large type books. | GSAFD: Western stories.
Classification: LCC PS3527.Y33 W57 2019 | DDC 813/.52—dc23
LC record available at https://lccn.loc.gov/2019017040

For

JACK BYRNE

Who has turned out—in our humble
estimation—one of the finest Westerns
we have seen in years!

CHAPTER 1

PORTENTOUS THINGS

THROUGHOUT that Southwest country one name stood head and shoulders above all others; a cognomen as far removed from most men's names as Timbuctoo from Ararat. That name was *Bufe Telldane,* whose owner was considered an enigma—the wastelands' greatest mystery.

All across New Mexico, West Texas and the Panhandle, tales of this man's daring furnished the raw materials for after-supper yarning round the campfires of the cow camps. His record smacked of legend, his deeds were things oft-told in whispers; but cursed or blessed he went his way, at once a danger and a warning.

There were those who swore by Bufe Telldane; a great many more swore at him—though seldom in his hearing. The tales were contradictory, the rumors considerably more so. You might be regaled at Laughing Horse with accounts of incredible daring, with tales of an open-handed generosity well nigh unbelievable; at Roaring Fork the accounts of this man's doings would make your stomach turn cold and crawl.

You might be told he came of a high-placed frontier family; that his father had been a ranger, his mother a Governor's daughter—yet there were those who as stoutly held him the scion of back-land brush-poppers, and cursed every time he was mentioned. It was apparent that no man knew. Nor could any say with certainty which town had been his birthplace, or what his education. You could not guess by his speech or dress, for these like his manners varied.

A corpse-and-cartridge occasion in a gambling dive at El Paso had first brought him into notice. The cartridges had been his—and the corpses, too! he'd departed without much leisure. And wisely; for people didn't know him then and would just as lief have swung him.

The victims had been prominent men.

He was a riddle that defied folks' solving, though all the country tried its hand and shook its head with dark scowlings. On one thing, though, most thinkers agreed—there was a woman back of him somewhere; only a woman could set a man, they said, to carving such hellbent trail.

Concerning Telldane, however, there were a number of fundamental truths that were subject to little twisting. During the late war, as boss of transportation, with the pay and rank of a major, it was known the man had gotten supplies and munitions through where no other could have done it. Five hundred mules had been dumped on him and the hardest task of the war; he had done it swiftly, ruthlessly and unforgettably, without comment, without parley. He could laugh in the face of bullets; often chuckled when there seemed no out—it were as though he invited death, defied it. Before the war, as scout under old Al Sieber—as Chief of Scouts under Crook, he had been repeatedly commended for bravery. He spoke Spanish and Apache fluently; was a crack shot, an all-round cowhand. As a deputy sheriff he had been the scourge of bad men. So much was known all across the land; the rest was garbled, uncertain. It was this 'rest' that kept folks talking.

It was hotter than hell's backlog and the pair in the creaking buckboard alternately cursed and mopped their faces. A wild, forbidding stretch of country, this land below the Mogollon Rim; a region of rugged untrammeled beauty that a man might travel a right long ways to find. These men had traveled a right long ways—all the way from Texas—but were not come hunting beauty.

An oddly assorted pair, these two; as alike in many respects as two peas in a pod, yet different as night from day in others. They had the same kind of lean, long-fingered hands, the same coiled-spring restlessness of movement; each had a cold, gun-barrel stare—the same edgy interest in his backtrail. But one was tall and one was short; the first was burly, the other slender. One was dressed like a dude and affected a dude's polished manners; the other was dressed like a saddle bum and had no manners at all.

Guy Topock, the tall man, kept twisting his thick red neck about, hard eyes showing the glint of approval. But the other, Andy Cooper he called himself, kept his bony face straight front, nursed the rifle in his lap and malignantly cursed the heat, the flies, and 'this goddam excuse fer a road!'

Topock chuckled. "Plenty room for your elbows round here, boy."

Cooper, unloading a stream of tobacco juice, allowed there had better be and announced himself fed up with being shoved around. "Reckon the ol' coot'll bite? How the hell much farther *is* it?"

"Three-four mile, I reckon. Great Grief! Twenty mile ain't far to go to get set up in the cow business—"

"Not if he sets us up, it ain't. It's a hell of a ways to go for—"

"He's set others up. Leastways we've heard he has."

After a while Cooper said: "Hope this damn rig holds together that long. Heat's enough to fry you! Reckon them rims'll stay on?"

Topock sawed on the reins and took a look. Climbing back he said: "They're still on now; but was we to run 'em through a creek—"

"Creek!" Cooper's laugh was rasping. "That's good! 'Creek,' says you! Why, the goddam frogs can't even swim! Where you goin' to find a creek?"

The tall man shrugged. "Reckon that's Wildcat Hill off there? Damn 'f I don't think it is," he said, squinting. "They said it looked like a mountain an' if that ain't a mountain—"

" 'Cordin' to that Payson crowd," Cooper said, "the best graze Kerwold's got is on that hill—and," he added, with a hand rasped across his jaw, "the on'y strings he's got on the place is that he's always used it. 'Tain't his at all. An' it's open to filin'—"

He looked at Topock thoughtfully.

Topock grunted; then suddenly swore. "Lookit that! Barb wire! By God, look there—goes clean out of sight!"

Cooper eyed the wire bitterly. "Thought you said this was free-grass country—"

"By God, I thought it was! First I ever heard of any wire round here—must be somethin' new."

They scowled toward where the fence was building off yonder across the hogback. Topock wheeled the horse. "Let's go over there an'—"

"Hey! Lookout fer that stump!" Cooper yelled; but his cry was a trifle tardy.

Topock, belatedly observing and trying to avoid the stump, swung the horse too far to the left—too far and much too abruptly. The ruts

11

of the road held the wheels like a lock, and the left shaft, with the animal's weight brought hard against it, snapped.

It fell with a clatter; and Cooper swore. "That's done it! By—"

"Aw, dry up!" Topock snarled, and got out. "There's some junk in the back of that seat there. See if you can find some wire—"

"Go find it yourself if you want it! *I* ain't fixin' no busted shaft in this heat—nor helpin', either! You busted it; go on an' fix it."

Topock's cheeks came around and his eyes jabbed a hard glance at Cooper. "All I asked—"

"I know what you asked—"

"Never mind!" Topock scowled; and looked across toward the fence-stringers. "I ain't so all-fired anxious to work up no lather, neither. There's some guys that'll do it—" He lifted his voice: "*Hey, over there—you birds by the fence! Wanta make some quick money?* That'll fetch 'em," he told Cooper and, leaning against the buckboard, rolled himself a smoke.

They saw one of the distant men detach himself from the wire and start toward them. "You can tell," Cooper sneered, "that guy's a hired hand by the hurry he's in to get here."

Topock grinned. "Prob'ly one of Kerwold's riders. Lazy crowd, from all I hear—treated too good, I reckon."

"When Kerwold sets us up," Cooper said,

12

"what-say we hire two-three of 'em away from him an' work the bloody hell out of 'em? Set the rest a good example an' show Sam Kerwold how a real cow outfit works—"

"Say-y! You know what?" Topock muttered, squinting across to where the newfangled red wire was going up. "Bet that ain't none of Kerwold's bunch at all! Lay you ten to one them fellas is nesters—betcha Kerwold don't even know about it!"

Cooper looked again and swore. "By the looks of this specimen I'd say you're right."

He referred to the man coming toward them, a heavy-set fellow with a stomach that was putting on weight. Stoop-shouldered he was, with a weathered face crisscrossed by wrinkles, with gnarled, rough hands and a four days' stubble of whiskers.

"From what I hear," Cooper muttered, "Kerwold's just the kind to lallydaddle round an' let a bunch of sod-turnin' riffraff move in on 'im."

The man from the fence came up with a good-natured, "Howdy. Havin' trouble, boys?"

"Damn shaft busted," Cooper growled, ignoring the greeting. Topock said: "Reckon you could fix it?"

The man rasped a hand across his cheeks, eyed the broken shaft, then looked at them and nodded. "Expect I could, like enough."

"Get at it then," Cooper growled at him. "Be

money in it for you if you can make it hold. This part of the Flyin' K range?"

The stoop-shouldered man looked around and nodded. "Have to go back to the wagon a minute an'—"

"How long'll it take to fix it?"

"Won't take long. You boys in a hurry?"

"Kind of," Topock answered. "How far off's the ranch?"

"Not above four mile, I reckon. Lays over behind that hill a piece."

While the fence-stringer pointed, Cooper's uncharitable glance took in his faded overalls, scuffed boots with their run-over heels, cheap shirt and sun-faded, floppy-brimmed hat. His own garb was not much better, but with an oath he spat across the singletree. "Damn nesters are comin' in everyplace."

The fence-stringer appeared to consider the remark. He said mildly, "That so?" and then, with a shrug: "Well, I'll get over an' fetch my cutters an' get you boys fixed up."

Cooper, biting off a fresh chaw, copiously splattered the harness tugs. He said loud enough for the departing man to hear: "If there's one breed of critter riles my bowels, it's the stinkin' hoeman tribe!" and spat again for good measure.

Elsewhere, and some hours later, twilight's obscuring haze bent down across the desert and

14

concealed the backtrail of the solitary horseman who had just come jogging out of it. Peering forward into the shadows of a wooded valley, this man sat moveless as a carven image; then, afterwards, turned his blue roan into a dry-bottomed wash that went angling upward into the timber's higher reaches.

He was bronzed, this man, baked dark by the glare; a tall, high-chested hombre with a tough and rugged face harsh-whipped by wind and weather. He rode stiffly in the saddle and probed each inch of the gloom-curdled way with a reticent, careful watching. Close acquaintance with violence had bred this care deep into him, and experience had confirmed its need.

At full dark this rider sat hunkered on his boot-heels high up in the green-clad hills, stare lost in the smoke of his campfire, a cold pipe gripped in his teeth.

From the tumbled slops at his left a stream lifted felted melody. The night was damp with an earthy smell and chill with the downsweeping breeze lifted off the yonder crags that, like a saw's edge, blackly etched themselves against the shine of stars.

The fire burned low. Neither blaze nor pipe was replenished.

Perhaps the rider dozed.

His chin was against his chest and all the lines of his face were loose, relaxed, when the gun's report laid its flat, sharp challenge across the night.

The man's tipped head came instantly up; the embers' glow showed his eyes alert and bright as steel's cold glinting. Like that he stayed for still, crouched moments.

Fog lay in the hollows now. It sparkled on his hat brim and was pale across his shoulders, wetly beading his rifle where it lay on the ground within quick reach of his hand.

For half a dozen heartbeats his shape held the embers' glow. Then he came, cat-soft, to his feet and eased himself back out of it. He took the rifle with him and, with features set like a mask, he got upon his saddled horse and for some further moments sat there with the track of some somber thinking grimly reshaping the lines of his cheeks.

This thinking determined his actions; all his impulses were subdued to its need. From out of the north that shot had ripped; it was eastward that he turned the roan. He sent it that way slowly with a flexing of his knees.

A scant two miles lay behind him when a tightened rein stopped the horse. Indian-still, intently grim, the man eyed the wink of lights coming out of a platter-like basin. A ranch lay there, or some crossroads hamlet.

It did not attract him, apparently, for he was turning the roan to round it when a second horse moved from the tree gloom.

A man's voice said: "If you're riding down to the store I'll ride with you."

"An' if I ain't?"

"But you are." A cold mirth ran that answer. "Of course you are—because why would a trail-tired hombre be passin' up a store an' lodgin' at one o'clock of the mornin'?"

CHAPTER 2

COLD TURKEY

IF THE old man heard what Cooper said, he gave it no attention. He had reached the fence and was starting for the wagon hitched a little way beyond, when Topock growled: "You might 'a' waited till the fool got out of hearin'."

Cooper sneered. "Hell! I never seen a squatter yet with enough peck to make a dungbug hustle."

He settled himself more comfortably and commenced paring on his fingernails with a long-bladed knife from his boot top. "Trouble with you is, you worry too much. Too damn careful. Too soft—that's what the matter is with you! It's why you won't never get no place. Hell! If it hadn't been for me—"

Topock snorted.

"I'll be runnin' cattle a long time after toughness has got you planted." He grinned at Cooper wryly. "*Your* trouble's packin' that stunt too far. One of these days—"

Andy Cooper grunted. "Horse hocks!" he sneered, and eyed his nails admiringly. "Horse hocks an' sparrow dung. I'll be pavin'—"

18

"You'll be pavin' the road to hell," Topock said, "if you don't quit bein' so contrary."

The old man returned with his wire cutters. He released the horse from the buckboard, led it off a piece and tied it. Picking up the broken shaft he fitted it to the stump and, shaking his head a bit, grunted. Setting the broken part down he drove a square nail into the shorter piece, using his pliers for a hammer. He took a pair of short boards from his pocket and, fitting the shaft to the stump again, placed one of the boards at either side of the break like a splint on a broken arm and stood thoughtful awhile, considering it.

"We ain't got all night," Cooper hinted.

Topock dug his ribs with an elbow, but the fence-stringer seemed not to notice. After a bit more of head-shaking and eying his work, he put the splints back into his pocket and again laid the shaft on the ground. He removed the nail he had driven and tamped in another nail closer to the stump. To this he fastened a length of wire securely. Fitting the shaft to the stump again, he put the splints back on and bound the whole methodically with wire, afterwards driving a couple more nails clear through the entire affair and flattening their ends on the farther side.

Everything seemed quite solid.

He stood back, surveying it with a critical eye while Cooper fumed and spluttered.

The old man, looking up, smiled at Topock. "I

expect that'll do it," he said, and got the horse back into the shafts.

Cooper snarled, "Give 'im 'is money an' let's git started. I'm drier'n a damn cork leg!"

"They got a right smart of water up to the ranch," the old man mentioned. "Just a minute now till I wrap this with a piece of hide so your horse won't—"

"To hell with the horse!" Cooper snarled. "Plenty more where he come from. Get out of the—"

"Here's your money," cut in Topock hastily, tossing the man a half dollar. "Much obliged. Do you know if old Kerwold's home?"

"Why-y—" The old man shoved back his hat. He scratched a hand along the side of his head and stood eying them somewhat dubiously. "You boys goin' up there to see Sam Kerwold?"

"Well, yes," Topock said, cutting off Cooper's sarcasm. "We was figurin' to—got a little proposition to put up to him."

"Ain't much sense goin' way up there, then." The fence-stringer told them soberly: "I'm Sam Kerwold. What's your proposition, boys?"

Topock stared. Cooper's jaw hung slack. Topock's face got red and he said uncomfortably: "Uh—er—Well, you see, Mister Kerwold, sir, I—we—er—We—"

"That's all right, boys. Just tell me what you wanted."

20

Cooper, whose tongue was swung from the middle, said: "We heard up at Payson how you been stakin' a number of fellas to a start in the cow business an'—"

"I'm afraid not, boys." Kerwold shook his head. "Sorry—but I don't hardly guess I could. Anybody that wouldn't know how to fix a wagon shaft wouldn't cut much figure in the cow business." He shook his head again. "No, I'm 'fraid not, boys. Runnin' cattle is pretty much work."

CHAPTER 3

WARP AND WOOF

THE MAN who had been camped in the hills could think of several good reasons why a fellow might not care to be the recipient of the yonder store's hospitality at one o'clock in the morning, but he was careful not to mention them.

He sat with inscrutable cheeks still turned toward the shine of light and with a twisted smile at last picked up his reins and at a slow jog sent his blue roan down the trail; and when they reached the store he got indifferently out of the saddle and looked at the other man briefly.

Store light, cutting the roadfront shadows, showed this second man to be garbed after the Mexican manner. He wore leg-clutching pants, short jacket and sash, with a chin-strapped sombrero for headgear. There was a mole's black spot at the right of his chin, and his stare showed bright and distrustful.

The man who had camped in the hills dryly mentioned, "We're here. Might's well go on in, hadn't we?"

A subtle change took place in the mounted

man's stare; then he shrugged and stepped out of the saddle. "Might's well," he said; and the two of them crossed the porch's warped planking and, still watchful, went into the store.

It was not the Ransome custom to stay open long after supper; but custom, for a lot of folk, was in the discard lately. A bit of research would have disclosed this change to have coincided with the arrival of a couple of Texans, though none took time for this effort. The change had come, was accepted.

Abe Ransome usually kept the store after nightfall for the hour or two it stayed open. But he was not a well man and here just of late his ailment had made itself felt more than usual; his daughter, Holly, had taken his chores and sent him off early to bed.

The first night she had charge of the store, one of the abovementioned Texans—Guy Topock was what the man called himself—had helped her while the time away with tales of his random travels. He had been a cattle buyer, he said, for Dallas' biggest packing house. The work seemed to have taken him far afield; his accounts of it were fascinating.

They'd been less so on the second night. The third night, after outstaying all other customers, he'd attempted to improve their acquaintance, to put it on a considerably more personal basis.

It had called up all Holly's tact and firmness to keep him in his place; by the time he'd finally left it had been nearly twelve o'clock.

But this fourth night was much the worst, she thought; it was after twelve already and Guy Topock still sat around grinning, with his hateful eyes doing things, she guessed, he'd an itch to have his hands doing for them.

About nine it had been when he'd drifted in; Juke Ronstadt had just ridden in at the time on his periodic trip for supplies. Old Juke was a kind of shiftless sort, a homesteader from over in Buck Basin. But a kind man and a husky one; and Topock had kept his jaw within bounds until after the old man left. Then the Texan, widening his grin, had got up and crossed to the counter.

"Gets kind of lonesome round here, don't it?"

Holly said, "I haven't noticed it."

"Sho. Like enough the reason is, there ain't been nobody round man enough to show you the difference."

His grin—the glint of his eyes—was a challenge. But Holly, throttling her resentment, was intending to change the subject when, grin widening, he leaned over the counter.

"Hold on now, girl—keep your shirt tail in; ain't no need you gettin' jittery." His hand shot out, just missing her as she backed off, stopped by the wall.

Her cheeks were white, her half-scared eyes wide and angry.

"Now what kind of way is that to act—fella'd think I was poison or somethin'."

He put the flats of his hands on the counter, firmly, as though of half a mind to jump it. She blushed suddenly and profusely at something she saw in his eyes. She was reaching behind her for something on a shelf when Topock decided to take it a little slower. After all there wasn't any hurry; she'd keep open till he left.

He was a slick talker, this Guy Topock; bland, suave and cunning—particularly with the ladies. He prided himself on his abilities in this direction. He said: "You ever thought of marriage, Holly?"

Holly's shoulders relaxed a little, but she kept her place by the wall. She shook her head. "Not much." Even in her own ears her voice sounded kind of queer.

Guy Topock thought so too, seemed like. A gloating look got into his eyes. He took a fresh grip on the counter and the knuckles of those hands were showing white when the porch planks creaked and across his shoulder Holly saw the rawboned shape of Pecos Gann.

Topock wheeled with his big-knuckled hands gone knotted. But the oath died sullenly on his lips when he saw who was in the doorway.

Gann's glance rubbed across him knowingly. "Warm night," Gann said.

He was a slat-shaped man with a lantern jaw and squinty, close-set eyes. A cud of tobacco bulged one cheek and a hank of grayish hair hung down across a corrugated forehead whose most significant feature was a long knife scar that began at his chin and lopped off half the left eyebrow. Gann had been a sheepman and still had a sheepman's habits, and when Holly spoke to him, asking what he wanted, his only answer was a surly grunt as he dropped down onto a nail keg from which he continued to eye Topock knowingly.

Topock's dark glance shifted but his talk was friendly enough. "It's a damn quiet night, if that's what you mean," he grumbled. He shrugged, let go a deep breath softly. "Deadest country ever I seen—your corral posts heir to dry rot yet?"

Gann said, "Not that I know of," and turned his speculative glance on Holly. She could almost *feel* the thoughts going through his head. She was wheeling away from them, red-cheeked, angry, resentful, when Gann said gruffly: "Where's that brother of yours at?"

It stopped her short. Then remembrance came with its need and she shrugged, went across the store.

She was rearranging stock on the far wall's shelves and the two men were swapping small talk like a brace of gamecocks sparring round, when horse sound drifted in again and a rider's

26

boots were presently knocking echoes from the porch.

It was her brother. His face was flushed, excited.

"Here's news!" he cried. "Clean your ears out, Gann. There's a hell's own smear of wagons comin' down Davenport Wash!"

All the lines of Gann's face deepened and he came half off the keg, with his black eyes showing ugly. "What's that?"

Ransome said: "Wagons! Twenty-thirty of 'em comin' down Davenport Wash!"

Gann sank back on his keg with a snorted oath. "Humph! Nothin' newsy to that," he said; but Holly noted that all expression was gone from his cheeks. His tone simulated indifference, but the look of his eyes didn't match it. "Been wagons," he said, "in that wash before. Headin' for the New River Mountains, prob'ly; goin' to stop at Ashfork for supplies. More homesteaders—that whole New River country's filled with 'em—"

"It may be," Tim Ransome growled, "but these ain't headin' that way. They're comin' down here, by grab, an'—"

"Hell!" Gann scoffed. "You better quit drinkin' that rattle juice Brill's puttin' out fer whisky."

"I'm tellin' you straight!" young Ransome scowled. He was a bony, peaked youth with the down of adolescence still satining his cheeks. Plainly the wish was in him to appear important.

27

Resentment edged his eyes at Gann's indifference. He said: "I got it right from Lou Safford. Lou's talked to 'em—they're askin' the way to Saint Clair Mountain—"

"Don't signify a thing," Gann told him, with a wink for Topock. "That trail connects with the road that goes up Seven Springs Wash. They'll be cuttin' over at Rackensack; take the ol' Fisk Mill road—"

"They *could*," Ransome said impatiently: "but they ain't. They give out to Lou they been tipped off this is all open range down here an' every man of 'em's aimin' to file!"

Gann rose with a sudden anger. "Then by God I know who told 'em," he said blackly. "That goddam Straddle-Bug Holcomb!"

Through the quiet that settled on Gann's remark came the humus-muted sound of falling hoofs. It came from the roadway yonder and drew all eyes to the door as spurs rasped across the porch planks.

Two men came in; Duarte Vargas, Kerwold's foreman, with his yellow stare sardonic, and a stranger. The stranger said to Holly: "If you've an extra bed round, ma'am, I sure could use it."

He was dark, above six feet, broad-shouldered, arrow straight. For some reason she herself could not define, Holly glanced at him again, more closely. The rim of his broad felt hat was

28

slashways pulled across his eyes and there was a conscious power in the way he carried himself; it was not a suggestion of cockiness or arrogance, but seemed rather the result of conviction—some knowledge not shared with these others. A faint smile was edging his lips.

The smile went away. He had observed her interest.

"Why," she said, "I—"

"Never mind," Guy Topock said, and came striding over. "You've got no room for him—see?"

The stranger looked at him casually, brows lifted in polite inquiry. His question seemed a natural one. "You're the proprietor?" he asked.

"Never mind," growled Topock harshly. "There ain't no room for you here."

Holly saw the amusement brightening Vargas's yellow stare, and wondered. Then her glance wheeled back to the stranger, found him eying her again. The set of his shoulders appearing to dismiss Guy Topock as of small importance. It did her good to see the look on Topock's face.

Then Topock's arm slashed out and whirled the new man round. "Damn you!" the Texan snarled. "When I'm talkin', you lis—"

He stopped like that with his stare gone wide, uncertain.

Holly stared at him wonderingly, for some of the ruddiness had gone from his cheeks and she saw no reason for it. The stranger, now that Topock's arm had fallen away from him, maintained a pose of careless ease; hipshot he stood, with thumbs hooked into his gun belt. A lazy smile was edging his lips, disclosing the shine of white teeth.

Topock took a long deep breath and his voice sounded strangely husky. "Say—ain't I met you before someplace?"

"Have you?"

Topock's odd stare held a moment longer. He said, more to himself it seemed than to the other, "I—I believe I have . . ."

To Holly it sounded like dust had got into his throat.

But the stranger appeared not to have noticed. "Well, perhaps you have," he murmured; and looking toward Holly again: "About that bed, ma'am—"

Whatever it was had bothered Topock appeared to have been shelved or forgotten. He said, cutting into the man's talk roughly: "I told you this place is full up. There's no room here—nor anyplace in this country—"

"You must be mistaken," the stranger said coolly. "This gentleman"—and his glance flashed at Vargas—"has invited me to stay for a while, and I've just decided I shall."

Holly's eyes followed Gann's and her brother's to Kerwold's foreman. Duarte Vargas said, grimly amused, "There was somebody killed in the hills tonight; I met this gent comin' out of 'em."

The place went queerly still. It were as though a mill had shut down and left its echo back of it.

The stranger's smile was regretfully for Holly.

"So I guess you've got a boarder, ma'am."

He leaned broad shoulders against a post and coolly shook tobacco from a sack into curled brown paper. With his teeth he drew the sack's strings shut; left hand thrust it in his pocket. A curling roll of the right hand's fingers made a perfect cylinder which his tongue's end licked while he considered their cocked expressions.

"Who was it?" Tim Ransome's voice had a shake in it.

The Flying K range boss shrugged. "I didn't notice." The polished brass of his stare stabbed its implication at the stranger.

"Why . . . I didn't notice, either," the stranger's drawl came blandly. "Never had much time for dead men—the live ones keep me too busy."

Gann said: "Tim, go get the marshal—"

Hot color stained young Ransome's cheeks. "Go yourself! I ain't no errand boy!"

"I will," Gann said, coming off his keg. But just then boot sound crossed the porch and stopped him; brought his head around to find the marshal framed in the doorway.

The marshal's raking stare found Vargas and he said tightly: "Juke Ronstadt was killed in

31

the hills tonight. What do you know about it?"

Vargas's glance hooked across to the stranger. "There's the gent you want to talk to."

"I'm talkin' to *you!*"

Duarte Vargas shrugged. Seemed to be a habit he had. "All I know," he said, "is I met this stranger comin' out."

"Whereabouts?"

"Near what's left of that corduroy road them fools—"

"How come *you* to be over there?"

Vargas met the marshal's stare brightly. "Why, I'll tell you, Lou. It ain't none of your goddam business."

Lou Safford moved a half step back and a long pale hand moved to cover his mouth as a racking cough bent and shook him. The face beneath his ash-blond curls was flushed and twisted as he pulled his head up after the coughing. The bit of cambric lifted from the breast pocket of his Prince Albert was looked at as it came from his lips before, with a shrug, he put it away. There was no expression in the wax-pale cheeks that he turned from Vargas to the stranger. His question under the circumstances was polite. "I'd admire to know what handle you are packing, friend."

"Bufford Dane," the stranger said.

"Dane, eh . . ." The marshal's left hand drummed a barrel top. "And what were you doing in the hills, Mister Dane?"

"Camping."

"About where?"

" 'Fraid I couldn't tell you. I'm a stranger to these parts."

"Hear any shots?"

"I heard one," Mister Dane said finally, slowly, carefully.

"Mind if I look at that gun you're packing?"

" 'Fraid I do." The stranger smiled.

Lou Safford didn't. He said sharply: "I'm marshaling this locality—"

"Glad to know you."

Safford's stare flashed a little narrow. He said no more about the gun. Instead he asked: "What can you tell me about that shot, Dane?"

"Nothing."

"Didn't you investigate?"

"It occurred to me that might be an unwise thing to do."

The marshal's stare revealed a subtle change. The silence thickened. The stranger's shoulders rested easily against the post; nothing about him showed perturbation. His eyes watched the marshal with a level directness that was baffling.

"Where you from?" Gann spoke abruptly; and Holly saw Topock's glance whip an instant look to the stranger's face.

"You might say," the man drawled, "I'm from Texas." And Lou Safford's pointed mention that

Texas was a 'pretty large place' brought only an indifferent shrug from him.

"Pretty large."

Topock put the thing to words. He said: "What part of Texas?"

"And what might be *your* interest, friend?" Dane's shoulders came away from the post. His tone was cold as gun steel.

A ruddy color stung Topock's cheeks and he drove a step forward with his big fists clenched and temper's warming in his eyes. "You're the one that's bein' grilled! An' you better—"

"That's right," Safford said. "I think—"

"Don't bother." Dane's eyes mocked them. "All you got to do is wait for daylight. Backtracking me will tell you all you need to know."

Topock sneered. "The wind—"

"Quit an hour ago," Dane said evenly. A cold amusement edged the stare he gave Topock.

Gann, who had been eying the stranger long and queerly, said abruptly: "*Geez!* D'you know—" and without bothering to finish the thought, drove a frantic hand at his gun butt. The thing was fast—fast and unexpected; but it wasn't quite fast enough. As the gun cleared leather light burst from the stranger's hip in a livid streak. The weapon was torn from the sheepman's hand, sent skittering across the floor, its clatter drowned in the reverberation Dane's gun slammed against the walls.

The group in the store stood frozen. No one moved but Gann, who was shaking his hand and cursing.

Safford, eyes flashing dark with anger, curtly said: "Put down that gun, Dane! I've a notion—"

"Sure," Dane smiled, "we all have," but the smile was glinting, mocking. "If notions was dollars, we'd be millionaires. The gentleman isn't hurt, you'll find. The slowness of his draw is to be commended—otherwise I might not have been able to take such deliberate aim. If all the parlor tricks are over now—and the young lady has a bed to spare—perhaps I'd better be sayin' good night. It's a little late and I'm sleepy."

CHAPTER 4

BLIND TIGER

BUFFORD DANE sat a long while upright on the bunk before he turned out the light and got into it.

This place was a kind of warehouse back of the storeroom proper. Long it was and narrow and perfumed with the mingled essence of many smells, much the strongest of which were those of cheap soap and sorghum. The dirt floor was cluttered with gear and with barrels; sacked grain and ground meals had their share of its space and the broad shelves lining three walls sagged with the weight of packaged goods and boxed stuffs. There was only one window, a narrow affair nailed tight as a drumhead and further secured by thick bars. It was a little remindful of a jailhouse, and Dane, connoisseur of atmospheres, permitted himself a dry smile.

But little mirth marked the indulgence and it was with a sigh—not entirely regretful—that he finally pulled off his boots and got into the bunk. His only other preparation before willing himself to sleep was the reluctant removal of gun belt and pistol—and the pistol he kept under his hand.

● ● ●

The sun was three hours high and the land commencing to broil again when Dane pulled on his boots and strode out into the store. An elderly man sat back of the counter with his bent glance on a book. Sunlight showed the gentleness of wrinkled, scholarly features; hardly the kind a man would look for in country wild as this.

Crossing the room Dane leaned against the counter, getting out sack and papers. The doors stood open and in this bright light the last of a quitting breeze playfully tousled the reader's hair; rattled paper on the counter. But the man read on, as unaware of wind's idle vagaries as he appeared to be of the stranger's presence.

Dane scratched a match on his Levi's and the man looked up, near-sightedly, reluctantly put aside the book and made a question of his glance. "Good morning."

"Mornin'," Dane drawled leisurely. "Good book, that—though a little on the tame side."

"You've read it, sir?" The man's eyes brightened. "A notable piece of work, sir—yes, indeed. There's genius in that fellow's pen—you've read his other works?"

Dane shook his head. "Don't have much time for readin'," he said dryly. "Uh . . . Would there be a place around here somewhere I could get a bite of breakfast?"

"Why—why, yes. Just a moment. I'll call my daughter."

But he didn't have to call her. She came through the door as he spoke. She had a smile for Bufford Dane; a smile he was starting to return when some dark thought appeared to cross his mind, straightening his lips out bleakly.

A moment's curiosity looked out of her level eyes. After which she said, "We've—Oh, pardon me! Father, this is Mr. Dane. Mr. Dane, my father, Abraham Ransome."

Dane reached across and shook the other man's hand; a thing he didn't often do, for shaking hands was dangerous. "Glad to know you, Ransome."

"Holly—" Ransome said, "Dane has read this book of Lytton's. Thinks it rather tame." He chuckled.

But Holly's eyes, briefly touching Dane's big pistol, showed an odd, half-wondering frown. But, whatever her thought, she shook it off. She said to Dane, "I've been keeping things hot. If you'll come with me . . ."

She turned away and Dane, reluctantly it seemed, followed her to the kitchen.

While she busied herself about the stove he let himself into a chair. He put his elbows gingerly on the oilcloth-covered table and roved a glance around. The room was plain, rather scantily furnished with rude things made in the country, but some magic of this tall girl's hands had made it homey, comfortable. A grudging approval briefly colored the stranger's stare.

He said, "About this fellow, Ronstadt . . . Have any enemies round here, did he?"

She said without looking up: "I never heard of any. He was a harmless old man. A homesteader from over in Buck Basin—"

"I see. A homesteader . . ." Dane said thoughtfully, and let his voice trail off.

Such times as Holly looked up from her work, the stranger's glance seemed always lost in consideration of some view beyond the window; but when she was not looking his regard was darkly on her, seeming to contrast her against some memory in his mind. It kind of bothered him, looked like, for the line of his face were somber.

He ate without comment and afterwards pushed his chair back, getting out the makings and twisting himself a smoke.

An odd stick, Holly thought of him, but somehow strangely attractive with his strong dark face and enigmatic stare. He had the look of a man who kept his horse at work. Her glance went oftenest to the big gun strapped at his hip; it seemed so much a part of him.

"What kind of jasper is this marshal—this Lou Safford?" he asked abruptly.

But she didn't get to answer.

39

Voice sound came from the store and on its heels the clump of boots. A deliberate, measured tread; and then Lou Safford was looking in at them, bony shoulders against the door.

He spoke with his glance on the stranger. "You'll be glad to know investigation backed you up, Dane. It don't seem hardly likely you could of had any part in Juke's killing. What are you going to do now? Figurin' to stay, or—"

"Why," Dane said, "I allow I'll stay. For a while, anyhow."

Safford nodded. "Kind of hoped you might see fit to." He paused, appeared to consider. His glance rubbed across Dane's pistol; calculation showed in the look. "Pretty fair with that gun, are you?"

Dane smiled dryly. "I expect I could make out to use it."

Safford said thoughtfully, "Be huntin' you up a job, I guess, eh?"

Dane shrugged. "Hard tellin'—ain't at all sure I'm goin' to stay, yet. Any of these outfits needin' a man?"

"I suppose Sam Kerwold might put you on." Safford said abruptly: "Sam's throwin' a party tonight—his daughter's just back from the east. Sort of birthday celebration. You might drop round; give you a chance to get acquainted—"

Dane said: " 'Fraid my talents ain't along that line."

40

Once again the marshal appeared to be communing with himself. He said abruptly: "I could find a use for a man like you . . ."

A quick light flashed in Dane's cold eyes. "You mean as deputy?"

Lou Safford nodded.

A wry grin parted the stranger's lips. "No, thanks," he drawled sardonically.

Lou Safford's glance was narrowed, odd. "What do you mean?"

"Trouble's buildin' up in this country—"

"Trouble?"

"Ain't a murder usually trouble?"

"Who said anything about murder?"

"A guy got killed in the hills last night. I didn't hear but one shot."

Lou Safford looked at him darkly. But all he said very quietly was: "That job will still be open tonight. You better think it over."

The barroom at Brill's was big—long, low-ceiled. A cluster of lamps, their yellow glare dimmed by tobacco haze, showed sections of the walls to be adorned with garish lithographs; the glass eyes of an elk's head, mounted above the back bar's mirror, leered out across Brill's bottled goods. Sweat and stale beer fumes mingled with the reek of whisky and from a rear room came the rattle of crap and chuckaluck games and the rumble of divers voices. Brill's place was known in the parlance of that day as a 'blind tiger.' It did

41

not mark a crossroads junction. It was crouched far back in the hills.

Apparently, though, it got its share of patronage. Any man was welcome so long as he packed no tin; and on this night the back room was pretty well filled with fellows, and a good many others were in the main room, ranged beside Brill's rough bar.

Two men, however, sat apart. Guy Topock and Andy Cooper. They had their heads together over a bottle, but they were not communing with any spirits. They were—as Cooper might have described it—'laying pipe.'

Topock was doing the talking, but every so often Cooper put in his oar—as now. "What," he said, grinning shallowly, "about this stranger, Dane?"

"What about him?"

"You don't need to wrinkle up your face at me," sneered Cooper. "Save it fer the women an' kids—they'll swaller it, mebbe." He laughed at the look in Topock's eyes. "That fella's got the Injun sign on you, boy!"

You could see that it bothered Topock. But all he said was, gruffly: "I'll take care of him when the time comes. Now quit your yappin' an' listen—you didn't leave any sign around that homesteader, did you? I mean, anything Lou Safford could use against you?"

Cooper snorted. "Yeah," he said sarcastically. "I scratched my name on his belt buckle!"

Topock ignored this pleasantry.

He said: "We got to work this quick, Andy—"

"I thought you was goin' to *tell* me somethin'!"

Topock watched Andy Cooper, a glinting anger in his eyes. "I don't know," he said, wickedly soft, "if that would be possible!"

"Horse hocks." Cooper grinned derisively. "Get on with it."

"What time you fixed it for that bunch of sodbusters to show up here?"

"Any time after tomorrow. Figgered we ort to have things—"

"Where'd you tell 'em to locate?"

"Wildcat Hill." Cooper grinned. "You said we wanted action—that'll fetch it."

"Jesus Christ, man!" Topock came half out of his chair. "That's the best graze Kerwold's got!"

"Sure—all the better, ain't it? The Flyin' K will hit them fools like a ton of lead."

"But, damn it! They'll have kids an' women with 'em—"

"All right; that won't hold the ol' coot back any. If they start tearin' up that grass—Hell," Cooper sneered, "he's got to smash 'em or kiss goodbye to the cow biz."

Topock looked at him a long half minute and finally shook his head. "You ought to sailed with Morgan—you'd made him a damn good mate. Ever stopped to think what's goin' to happen if any of them women or kids git hurt? They'll have the troops down here s' quick it'll make your head swim!" Topock ran a shaking hand through his hair and swore.

Cooper's lip curled. But he had the wit to keep his mouth shut. He understood Guy Topock pretty well; knew to a fraction just how far he could prod the man—knew that limit had been reached.

"Look," he said after a moment. "The plan is to get these hoemen to prod Kerwold's crew into gunplay—all right. Beddin' 'em down on Wildcat Hill will do it. He'll tear into 'em like the devil beatin' tenbark—prob'ly burn up half their wagons for a starter. Fine! that gets the ball to rollin'. That's what we been waitin' for, ain't it? Sure! All right; we hit back at Kerwold—cut his fence, burn a couple line camps, mebbe; kill three-four of his men. Surer'n hell he'll lay it onto them homesteaders. When the smoke clears off there won't be any Flyin' K—won't be any homesteaders, neither. We step in an' take the whole works over. What the hell could be sweeter'n that?"

Guy Topock remained without speaking so long that Cooper shifted uneasily. He poured himself another drink and when he picked the glass up it was his left hand that curled around it; his right was at the table edge, short inches from his gun.

Topock ironed the scowl from dark features,

but anger still thickened his voice. He said: "You got a ridin' crew lined up?" and Cooper nodded.

"Got eight-ten fellas—all of 'em good with rifles. It wasn't no chore; these small-spread ranchers round here ain't wastin' no love on Kerwold. Been expandin' too fast—they're scared of him, 'fraid they're goin' to be gobbled. I—"

"Did you sign on Holcomb?"

Cooper said "No," reluctantly. "Wouldn't talk one way or the other." He said with his tone turned thoughtful, "May have a little trouble with him."

Topock growled, "Never mind. Can you get these boys in a hurry?"

"Any time you want 'em."

"Where's young Ransome?"

Cooper's head jerked a nod at the back room's closed door. "He's in there buckin' Brill's games. Want him?"

Topock's glance was considering. "No," he said finally, "not now. You fixed it up with Brill to take his I.O.U.'s? . . . Good. I got a—"

"How you goin' to work Safford?"

Some secret thought crooked Topock's lips. He said, "Your worry's handlin' Vargas. That guy has got ambition—"

"I got a handy cure for ambition." Cooper suggestively patted his gun. "You goin' to Kerwold's shindig?"

45

"Yeah." Topock looked at his watch and got up. "Keep those fools well heeled with money." He tossed a buckskin sack on the table and ten minutes later went out.

CHAPTER 5

"I WANT THAT STEALIN' STOPPED!"

THERE were five people enjoying Sam Kerwold's spiked punch in the Flying K's long living room when Bufford Dane brought Holly into it. There was Sam Kerwold and his daughter, a neighboring rancher, Lou Safford and one of the men Dane had seen in Ransome's store the night before.

An ironic smile disturbed the set of Safford's lips as he bowed, but he vouchsafed no remark and Holly, after returning the greetings of Sam and Sam's daughter, said to Kerwold: "Mr. Kerwold, I would like you to meet Bufford Dane who is staying at the store for a while."

Sam Kerwold held out his hand and Dane shook it, after which Kerwold said: "Like to have you meet the guest of honor, Dane—My daughter, Jane."

Holly, looking up at Dane, saw the sudden tightening of his shoulders; observed the way the long hands, until then loose-hanging at his sides, went oddly white about the knuckles. With a catch of breath she stabbed a look at Jane.

She had known Jane rather well before the latter had gone East to school. But someway this was not that Jane; this girl was different, not merely more mature, more dignified and graceful, but different in her habits of thought—different of mental viewpoint. Holly sensed other changes not so easily labeled.

As Holly looked at her, Jane went a half step backward, stood with cheeks gone pale, her startled gaze incredulously fixed on Dane. It was only for a second Jane stood with feelings naked, but Holly saw, and her swift, half-vexed interpretation was that these two, Jane and the stranger, had met before.

Kerwold's daughter must have recalled her surroundings then, for her chin came up and with strengthening color she said quietly, "How do you do?" but did not offer her hand, nor, apparently, did Dane expect her to.

It seemed to Holly that Dane's bow was a trifle elaborate and she thought to read the glint of a malicious humor in his glance as he said coolly, "I'm fine enough, thank you," and, turning to grin at Kerwold, asked: "Are we celebrating the prodigal's return?"

Kerwold had been eying Dane a little oddly, almost searchingly. But he chuckled at the question. "You might call it that, I reckon, though I haven't readied any fatted calf—and may not get to," he added more soberly, "if somethin' ain't soon done about these rustlers."

"Something's *being* done," Safford said, a little quick with his answer. "Dane, here, is figuring to help me get the deadwood on—"

"He means he *hopes* I am," Dane answered, grin showing the cold white teeth of him. "As a matter of fact, I've about decided not to take on that chore. Havin' lead thrown at you from behind every rock and pinon ain't hardly my idea of a happy life."

Lou Safford frowned. "That mean you're turning down my offer?"

"I'm afraid it does."

Lou Safford said: "I might have known a man too careful to investigate a shot, like you done in the hills last night, hadn't sufficient guts to be a deputy."

They were a little shocked, those others, by the marshal's plain-put words. Sam Kerwold looked embarrassed, but the stranger took it cool enough. His tipped-up cheeks revealed a cold amusement; but as he seemed about to comment, Guy Topock came through the door and his bold stare picked Lou Safford out immediately. "What's the latest on that hold-up, Safford? Got a line on the killer yet?"

It was a good entrance; he could not have made a play that would have grabbed attention quicker. All eyes wheeled, and Pecos Gann, who had been about to say something, stared with his mouth

49

left open. "What hold-up?" Kerwold said, quite plainly startled. And "What killing?" Pring, the other rancher, said.

Lou Safford scowled. "It ain't generally known yet," he admitted, "but the Phoenix stage, coming west from Globe, was stopped this evening just above Horse Mesa—"

"The driver," Topock cut in, "was killed and the strong box emptied of every last nickel in it!"

"Reason I haven't mentioned it," Safford said, with a malevolent look at the Texan, "is because I didn't want to throw cold water on the party. I've got men all through the hills hunting sign—"

"Haven't heard anythin' then yet, eh?"

"Not yet," the marshal said curtly; and Kerwold stared at his boot tops gravely.

"How'd you come to hear of it?" Pring asked Topock, and the Texan grinned. "I was there when that fool coffee drummer come tearin' in with the stage." He laughed at a sudden memory. "His eyes was bugged out like marbles."

Plainly Safford did not care to discuss the hold-up and presently the talk, turned into other channels, became more general. Dane brought her a glass of punch and dipped another for himself, and Pring, leaning forward, asked if he'd care for a riding job at sixty-five and found. Dane, without committing himself, said he'd keep the offer in mind.

Pring, Holly told him later, was owner of the Double Bar Circle. "They say Sam Kerwold helped him when he was starting six-eight years ago; they're great friends," Holly mentioned and, watching Dane carefully, said: "Gus used to be pretty much interested in Jane before she went off to school—everyone figured they'd get married sure."

But Dane showed nothing beyond polite interest; and then Guy Topock came striding over and Dane, excusing himself, said he guessed he'd go have a smoke.

Dane was not long on the veranda when a voice said from the shadows beyond the rail: "Vergas told me how he herded you into Ransome's store last night."

It was Kerwold's voice, guarded but unmistakable.

Dane did not move to join the Flying K owner, but at once dropped his unfinished smoke to the floorboards and put a foot on it. "Yeah." He said: "Damn fortunate, as things worked out, but kind of odd."

"How you mean, odd?"

"For one thing, what was he doing there?"

"Why—ah—just what the hell you getting at?"

"Well," Dane's voice was considering. "He came out of the trees like he'd been there handy, waitin' for something."

There was a moment of silence. The wind made a lonely sound.

Kerwold said abruptly—sharply, almost: "Are you insinuating—"

"Never mind. Let it ride," Dane answered gruffly. "I can take care of myself, I reckon. Did you tell him you had sent for me?"

"Hardly." Kerwold's tone was nettled. "I didn't tell him anything."

"Good!" Dane said, and after a moment: "Don't. You know my style—a lone hand always. Only way to get anything done. Your letter didn't tell me much; what are you up against here?"

Kerwold took a long time answering. He said then grimly: "As God's my witness, Bufe, I'm damned if I know. I been expandin' a little lately; buyin' up small holdings here an' there—I need more range and the free grass days are done. Homesteaders comin' in everywhere; there's goin' to be fences, pastures, farmin'—as a matter of fact, I'm fencin' myself—got to. It isn't makin' me popular. The small-spread outfits think I'm fixin' to hog the water, and in a way they're right; man that's got water's goin' to control this country and I'm not goin' to be froze out or dictated to by no passle of weed-bendin' hoemen. I—"

"You're not fencin' open range?"

"No. But I'm buyin' it fast as I can—I've got to to protect myself. I can see what's comin' all

52

right. I don't blame these little fellers—I started that way myself—"

"Any your men filin'—?"

"Sure; every one of 'em is. Soon's they prove up, I'll take over—they'll not lose anything; I've agreed to pay them five hundred dollars apiece, over and above their wages. They wouldn't make nothing of it anyway—not cut out to be farmers. There ain't one of 'em that'll do anything he can't do from a saddle; they'd feel insulted if I asked 'em to string fence. I'm doin' all that myself—me an' the cook."

"What did you want me to do?"

Kerwold hesitated. He said suddenly, angrily: "Put the fear of God in these rustlers before they rob me blind!"

"What's the matter with Lou Safford?"

"Nothing—that I know of. But he's only one man; he can't cope with everything."

Dane might have pointed out that he, too, was only one man. But instead he said, "You looked kind of funny when that guy Topock was blowing off about the stage hold-up—have anything on it?"

Kerwold swore, quietly but with undoubted warmth. "Two thousand dollars cash comin' from the bank at Globe!"

Dane pursed his lips in a soundless whistle. "What was the big idea?"

"The Government Land Agent at Prescott has

announced that a big jag of land just east of here, startin' at Wildcat Hill, is goin' to be let on a five year lease—"

"You mean this land's to be bid on?" Dane interrupted.

"Yeah," Sam Kerwold said morosely. "Wednesday, at Fort McDowell—"

"Why there?"

"Don't ask me—some kind of politics, like as not. But you ain't got the picture yet. This land's goin' to be bid on Wednesday *if an' providing that* no homesteads have been taken up on it in the meantime. If one homesteader stakes a claim, the bidding's off—"

Dane did whistle this time, softly. "Anybody else interested in this jag of land?"

"Yeah—three-four big outfits interested. Pring, for one, would like to get it, though I don't reckon Pring will bid knowin' how bad I need it. Then there's the Wagon Wheel, Straddle Bug, an' Blane's Four Bars off the other side of New River. Them three's pretty sure to bid—"

"Ain't you fellows worried some of these little spreads'll be sendin' someone to file—"

"They'd do it quick enough if they dared," Kerwold said, "but they don't. We've got along all right so far, but I guess they know how long they'd last if they tried anything like that."

"Always the chance of real sod-busters turnin' up, though, and—"

"I know that." Kerwold's voice showed his worry.

"How come you're wantin' this lease so bad?" Dane asked; and Kerwold told him.

"I'm sold too deep into next year's deliveries," he said grimly. "I'm committed for a sight more Basin-fed beef than I can show unless I get this Wildcat land—God damn it, Bufe! that country'll feed more'n fifty head to the section."

"That good, eh?"

"You know it!"

"How does it happen you ain't wangled this—"

"Hell, it ain't been open till this month!"

"An' there's three more days before the bidding, eh?"

Kerwold said "Yeah," morosely. "I tell you, Bufe—"

"That's the third time you've called me that in five minutes. For the love of God, Sam," Dane said sharply, "get a hobble on your jaw. I'll not be no use to you dead."

"Sorry." Kerwold's tone was short. He would have said more, it seemed, but Dane cut swiftly in:

"You haven't said yet what it is I'm supposed to do. You spoke of rustlers—got any idea who they are?"

Kerwold said almost inaudibly, "I couldn't prove anything—"

"But you've got a lot of ideas?"

Sam Kerwold said impatiently: "I got some notions. You better make your own mind up. On evidence got by yourself."

"Well, tell me this: Who you think's behind it?"

"Rather you'd find that out someplace else, too."

Dane's eyes narrowed. He wished he could see Sam Kerwold's face, but this gloom was like a blanket. "You ain't givin' me much help."

Sam Kerwold's voice was reticent. "I know it. You'll have to work this out yourself—I know it sounds kinda lowdown-like, to bring a man three hundred miles to help you out of a jackpot an' then make him play it blind. But that's the way it's got to be."

There was a finality in the way he put it that precluded further argument. That was the proposition. Dane could take it or he could leave it.

He said dryly: "I always did do things the hard way. Would you mind tellin' me, Sam, what you're wantin' done with these fellows after I've spotted 'em?"

"I told you once I want the fear of God put into 'em!" The cattle baron said it harshly, smashed a fist against the porch rail. "I want that stealin' stopped—stopped permanent and pronto. How you do it's up to you."

CHAPTER 6

Grim Challenge

LONG moments after Kerwold wheeled away, Dane stood there in the porch gloom, silent, thoughtful. It was apparent enough from Kerwold's talk what was happening, or about to happen, here. An old familiar pattern, as familiar to Bufford Dane as the shiny creases of his saddle. Forces were at work here—greed and jealousy and fear. Someone had his knife out, someone determined to smash Sam Kerwold and everything he stood for. Flying K was headed out—unless drastic steps were taken. Only one thing could save it. Force must be met with force.

That Kerwold was feared and hated was not surprising to Bufford Dane; the surprise was that he'd got this far without somebody gunning him. There was nothing wrong with Kerwold—with what he'd thus far done; he was a part of the accepted system just as his enemies and what they aimed to do were part of that system. It was dog eat dog; rugged individualism; competition at its best. So long as competition endured, so long would these things happen. It was the way—the way of this time and place.

Bufford Dane was a man of few illusions and what few he owned had long since been discarded. He saw things as they were—or most things. Sam Kerwold's problem was an open book, a thing he knew page for page. There were just two courses possible. No halfway measures counted; you must take the one or the other. You could fold your hands and do a lot of wishful thinking, or you could grab a gun and start smashing things.

Sam Kerwold had not called on him to sit with folded hands.

Jane Kerwold was playing the piano, the only one in the country. At considerable expense this instrument had come a weary way; it was a facet of Sam Kerwold's pride, like his daughter, like his ranch. He liked to hear it played and enjoyed watching others hear it. Jane Kerwold had a light, sure touch that made listening a pleasure.

Bufford Dane was probably the only one not affected by the music.

Holly, covertly eying him, was sure he did not hear it. The somber look of his burnt-dark cheeks was not produced by Jane's melodies; it was the result—if Holly were any judge—of thinking, of a thinking wholly unpleasant.

His eyes veered, observed her interest; the

dark cheeks locked his thoughts away. He said, calmly casual, "Been a long time since I heard that song," and shifted his regard to the ceiling.

But when Holly looked again she found him studying Safford. There was a darkness in his glance that set her own mind probing. Who was this Bufford Dane? She had asked herself that thing before. Where had he come from? What lay back of him that made his glance so wary?—his step so cat-soft quick?

There was a mystery about him that attracted her. His strong, dark, enigmatic face bespoke a man who did things—who had done some things, she guessed, which would not bear open talk about. The baffling blue of his eyes said so; the reticent slant of his cheeks.

She wished she could know his story. That somewhere along his backtrail that story had crossed Jane Kerwold's, Holly felt certain. She could not forget the girl's startled look—the stiffening of Dane's shoulders when Sam Kerwold had introduced them; that is to say, when they'd first taken stock of each other.

Holly's regard of Jane's back had something of envy in it. There was a look about Dane's features, about the set of his broad, sloped shoulders, that warned he was not a fit subject for trifling. Yet Jane must have trifled—or had she? What other interpretation could be put upon their silence regarding that undoubted previous acquaintance? That both regretted it was obvious; but whose had been the fault? *Had* Jane trifled with him, or—?

Holly looked at Dane again. His regard was on Jane Kerwold now, faintly aglint with a cold amusement; yet back of that sardonic look Holly thought to detect other and darker things—a bitter cynicism, surely.

And then her thoughts and reflections were shattered. A sharp hail rode the night; horse sound pounded the yard's adobe, cutting through Jane's playing, breaking it. There was an outside mutter of voices, booted feet thumped the porch boards and a hatless man came wild-eyed through the doorway, roved a stare while he caught his breath and said to Kerwold hoarsely: "There's wagons on Wildcat Hill an' all that fence we run below is ripped plumb out of the ground!"

CHAPTER 7

RUBBED OUT

"NO MAN," Andy Cooper snarled, "can use me like Sam Kerwold has an' not git paid back for it!"

They were in a rear and private cubbyhole at Brill's; just the three of them, Brill, Andy Cooper and Topock. Topock's face was white. He was mad clean through. Not a hot, tumultuous anger that would spend itself in abuse or in some fierce exchange of blows, but a cold and deep, controlled kind of rage that put a chill up Brill's arched back.

He put the back against a wall. He wanted no trouble here, no grabbing after guns. "Now look—" he said. "Take it easy, boys; that ain't no way for you to talk. Two wrongs never made a right. Let's talk this o—"

Topock's voice went through that talk to strike at Cooper like weighted fists. "Never mind bringin' Kerwold in! We're talkin' about that switch you pulled. When I tell a man how to do a thing, that's the way I want it done, by God! What was the idea you bringin' them sodbusters in ahead of time?"

Cooper's bony face showed ugly. He made no reply, but sat there like a sullen lump and glared like he would put a curse on Topock.

Brill tried his hand again. "I think—"

Topock said: "Keep out of this, Brill!" and his black intolerant stare bludgeoned Cooper like a maul. Rage jerked at him, tore wild words from his mouth. The names he applied to Cooper were things no man would ordinarily take.

But Cooper took them, silently and sullenly. And when his pardner had run out of breath, Cooper thrust one chap-clad leg across the other and spat with a glance like agate.

"It seems to me," Brill mentioned dryly, "you're wastin' a lot of words on somethin' that ain't worth twenty. What difference does it make *when* your sodbusters get there, just so it's ahead of the bid-day?"

But Topock ignored him. He shoved his voice at Cooper wickedly. "There's just one boss to this outfit, hombre—just one, an' that one's *me.* Never do another thing without you ask me first. You hear?"

"I hear," Cooper said, and his lip curled as Safford's voice drew Topock's glance to the door.

Topock said "Well!" harshly as Safford closed the door. "Let's have it. What did Kerwold do to them wagons?"

Safford's wheeling glance was odd and he took plenty of time with his answer. He said softly, thoughtfully, "Kerwold hasn't touched the wagons, hasn't molested the homesteaders either. I can't think what's holdin' him. He told me he expected me to find out who was responsible for that mess someone made of his wire."

They stared at him blankly.

"Mean to tell me," Topock ripped out, "he's goin' to leave them wagons bedded down on Wildcat—that he aims to let them homesteaders *file* it?"

Safford nodded. "That's the way it looks."

"But—that's crazy, man! He *can't*! He'd never *dare* to! It's a trick, I tell you—a damn trick to get you out of the way! He's *got* to have that lease to meet next year's commitments."

The marshal shrugged. "All I know is what I told you. He ain't botherin' the wagons."

"Not botherin' 'em now, mebbe," observed Brill thoughtfully, "but that ain't sayin' he won't—You know well as I do, Lou, he's got to have that lease."

"I know he had some money comin' on that stage that got stuck up." Safford's stare was solidly on Cooper. "You didn't happen to work that, did you?"

"Sure," Cooper sneered. "With my ol' man's gun I did it!"

He chucked his chew in a corner, bit another from his plug. "What give you the idee *I* stuck it up?"

"That coffee drummer's description—"

Cooper snorted. "How long you been a star-packer?"

"What's that got to do with it?"

"Nothin'—only you ort to know how reliable a eye-witness's guesswork is—"

" 'F I thought you was tryin' to cut a rusty, I would sure eye-witness *you,*" Safford said mighty quiet-like; and turned back to face Guy Topock. "No, the Ol' Man never s' much as put a finger on those wagons, Guy. Just sat there—"

"Mad, though, wasn't he?"

"He might of been," Safford said; "but if he was, he sure covered up good. Never made any threats—"

Brill said: "I bet Duarte Vargas did!"

The marshal nodded. "Yeah, he sounded off considerable. But when he got all through, Old Sam said mighty earnest-like: 'No you're not, boy—not while you're roddin' *my* spread.' " Safford grinned. "Vargas shut down like a grist mill."

Topock said: "What you figure on doin' about Kerwold's wire?"

Safford puffed his cheeks out, hauled a stogy from his pocket. As he bit the end from it, his eyes held a dry kind of humor. "If I could guess," he said, "who was responsible, I might figure to oblige Sam by making an arrest. But shucks— ain't hardly a man in this basin won't paw sod

64

when you mention wire. Be like hunting a needle in a haystack."

Cooper guffawed.

Brill, who was not a talking man, spoke then. Mostly he kept his mouth shut and let his eyes reward him, but the enigma of Kerwold's attitude for one time bothered him out of this caution. He said with his beefy jowls turned fretful: "What you s'pose Sam's got up his sleeve? You don't reckon he *wants* to see them homesteaders filin' Wildcat, do you?"

It was a new idea. The expressions of these others showed it. Safford's chalk-pale face turned thoughtful and Topock rolled his shoulders as he swung with a sudden curse; but it was Cooper's tricky head that grasped the implication first and he slammed off his stool with twisted cheeks, smashed a hot wild look at the others.

"By God, Brill's got it!" His fist struck the table with a force that made the bottle jump. "It's plain as paint—the slick ol' bastard!" He raked a stare at Topock. "Know what he's goin' to do? By grab, *I'll* tell you! He's goin' to let them weedbenders file an' then get his lease from *them!*"

"You're loco!" Safford grunted.

Brill said bewilderedly, "But that's foolish, Andy. He can't lease from them—"

"Why can't he?" Cooper's slitted stare was bright. "Why can't he?" he repeated. Then harshly: "It's the smartest thing he *can* do! It cuts out competition; knocks that auction out of the picture—Hell! *he can lease that land from them homesteaders for half what a bid will cost him.*"

A cold, grimly thoughtful silence clamped down upon that cluttered room.

Safford's considering stare saw Topock's glance flick across to Brill; saw Brill nod slowly. "It could be," Brill said uneasily. "What the devil we goin' to do?"

Topock said, "Them other boys will go hog wild when they find what Kerwold's up to—"

"That ain't helpin' us!" Cooper snarled. "I say—"

"Now wait," Topock said. "Keep your shirt tail in. Let's figure this out a bit. It might be we could—"

"It looks," Safford dryly mentioned, "like bringing those squatters in wasn't near as smart as you figured. If this lease guess is right, Sam's got us blocked."

Bright flecks coalesced in Cooper's glare. He said with a wild beast's anger: "By God, I'll lead the boys on a raid that'll un-block us pronto! I'll—" He broke off as cold air knifed the room, set the smoke haze swirling bluely. Bony shoulders wheeling, he looked toward the door.

Duarte Vargas stood in the opening with a hard grin edging his features. There was an ironic glint in his dour yellow stare as he closed the door back of him softly.

A rope-calloused thumb stroked the mole on his chin; the look of his eyes froze them rigid.

There was this moment of strained, brittle silence. Then "Spit it out, damn you!" Cooper shouted.

"They're gone."

"Who—who's gone?" Topock's eyes showed startled.

"Them precious nesters you brought in."

Cooper's jaw hung slack. Brill, too, showed disbelief.

Safford said: "You mean they've cleared out?"

"Lock, stock an' barrel. There ain't a wagon left on Wildcat Hill—"

"What the hell are you talkin' about?"

Cooper came cat-footed across the room, fists clenched, stare smashing at Vargas.

But Kerwold's foreman stood his ground. "Just what I said. Wheel an' hub. They've gone—there ain't a plow-chaser left on that lease."

The silence dried out, got sharp and hard.

Brill bewilderedly said: "Where've they gone to?"

Vargas shrugged. "Your guess is good as mine. The sign led toward the New River trail but—"

"Did Kerwold scare them out?"

"No, Lou, I don't reckon he did—"

Cooper scowled. "He bought 'em out, then!"

But Vargas shook his head. "I don't think Sam even spoke to them. They were there when the party broke up and they were there when the outfit turned in—scattered all across that slope. Must have been around twelve when I left Sam at the veranda. I turned in like the rest; but soon's I was sure they was all cuttin' wood, I slipped out an' saddled up—"

"What for?"

Vargas met Cooper's look with an easy grin. "Call it a hunch if you want. Anyway, I saddled up and went over there—"

"You was goin' to play 'em a tune on your mouth harp, mebbe?"

Topock said exasperated: "Shut up, Andy—let him get the thing told!" And to Vargas: "They was gone, eh?"

Vargas nodded.

"You were saying something about New River."

"Yeah. I was sayin', Lou, the sign appeared to point that way—"

"Appeared?" Brill said.

"Uh-huh. You see," Vargas smiled, "somebody had rubbed it out."

CHAPTER 8

GUY TOPOCK

THERE was something wicked, something wild and ugly in the swing of Cooper's shoulders as he came round the table on cat-soft feet and started for the door.

"Where you goin'?" Topock glared.

"After them goddam squatters! I'm goin' to find out where they went an' I'm—"

"You're goin' to stay right where you are. Safford's the man to handle that—"

Cooper's uncharitable look raked Safford intolerantly. He said nothing. He was started for the door again when Topock's hand clamped hold of a shoulder, spun him round. "Get back on that stool an' stay there!"

Across three feet of piled-up silence the Texans eyed each other. Cooper's face was twisted, scowling; Topock's stare was like spilled ink. Then abruptly Cooper wilted, went sulkily back to his stool.

There was a new respect in Safford's stare. Brill's looked odd, uncertain, nervous; the glint of Vargas's remained unchanged. Safford said, "You want me to—"

"I want you to get on the trail of those home-steaders pronto. I want to know where the hell they're goin'; or if they've got there, where they went." Rage still thickened Topock's talking. He drew a deep breath and said more quietly: "Don't ride up to 'em. Don't talk to them an' don't let them know you've followed 'em—don't let them see you at all. When you've found out where they're headed, come back an' tell me. Don't come back without you do."

Safford nodded, wheeled through the door. Kerwold's foreman closed it back of him.

Brill, troubled glance on Topock, said: "Think you ought to trust him that way?"

"I don't trust nobody," Topock said, and his look at Brill was a warning. He put that glance at Vargas then. "What's Gann got against Hol-comb?"

Duarte Vargas's eyes showed a faint surprise. "How'd you know—?"

"I'm askin' the questions," Topock snapped. "What's he got against him?"

The expression of Vargas's cheeks changed subtly. "Goes a long way back," he said, and paused as though considering. "Gann used to be in the sheep business. Got to nursin' the idea once he'd like to see sheep in this basin; didn't figure he could cut it by himself, so he propositioned Holcomb—tried to get Straddle Bug's backing. Said they'd split profits fifty-fifty, him to furnish

70

the sheep an' Holcomb to furnish assistance if the going got a little rough. Holcomb turned him down flat; said if he brought sheep into this country Straddle Bug would undertake to kill 'em off fast as they showed. Holcomb," Vargas added suggestively, "is one of the gents Sam Kerwold set up in business."

Topock stood silent a moment. "That all Gann's got against Holcomb?"

"Not quite. Short time after that some of Gann's best beef started takin' sick an' one night somebody fired his range, an' a little bit later two of his stacks was burned an' he come near losin' his buildin's. It's never been proved Holcomb had any part in it, but Gann's always blamed him for it."

"How did it get out Gann wanted to bring sheep into the country?"

"Holcomb told it—or one of Holcomb's outfit. I ain't sure which. Gann lays it to Holcomb. I know Holcomb offered to buy Gann out."

"Nothing come of it, eh?"

Duarte Vargas shrugged. The glint of his eyes turned ironic. "Three-four months after that, Holcomb found two of his waterholes poisoned. It got around his crew laid it onto Gann, but Holcomb never done nothing about it—never would talk about it, either. Fact is, he never talks much about anything. Got a rough lock on his jaw, I guess—lives all the time under his hat."

Topock said to Vargas: "Next time you run across Holcomb, mebbe you better let drop Gann's throwin' his jaw round about him. Spread it on thick, tell him Gann's talkin' about a shoot-out next time Holcomb crosses his track."

By the wall, Brill's glance went roundly inquiring. "You figurin' to start things between them two again?"

"Long as these outfits stand pat," Topock said, "we can't do anything with them. Get 'em at each other's throats an' half our work's done for us." He looked Brill over thoughtfully. "You might start the word to circulatin' that Gann's talkin' sheep again. And next time Gann comes in here it might be a good idea for him to get the notion Holcomb's makin' war talk."

Vargas said with his eyes showing crafty, "Willow Creek Wally's a man you can use. He hates Ab Holcomb like castor oil—used to be Straddle Bug's foreman—"

Topock said: "This Wally's in your string, ain't he, Andy?" and Cooper nodded sullenly.

"What about Pring?" Brill said.

"I was comin' to that," Topock nodded. "You might sort of hint to Kerwold, Vargas, that Gus Pring's borrowin' heavy to get that Wildcat lease—"

Kerwold's foreman shook his head. "That's out. Sam won't listen to a thing against Pring—"

"Never mind. Mention you heard it anyway.

72

Suspicion's the best weapon we've got. Get enough of these outfits uneasy an' the rest'll be a cinch. The way to lick a game like this is to use every card you can get hold of."

Vargas's glance, while Topock was expounding this philosophy, showed far back in its depths the glint of a secret amusement. But his cheeks were darkly sober when he said, "What about this new man, Guy? You forgettin' him?"

"What new man?"

"That fella Dane I brought in last night."

"What about him?"

"I don't know." Vargas's tone was evasive. "Seemed like a pretty cool customer—I was sort of wonderin' if we could use him—"

"I'll take care of him," Topock answered flatly. "You mind what I told you. Get to work on Holcomb and Kerwold. Brill—you get Pecos Gann stirred up, and Andy," he said with a look at Cooper, "you go fetch Willow Creek Wally. Him an' me is due for a talk."

"Uh—just a minute," Brill said; "I thought—"

"Thinkin' ain't in your line, Brill. You just leave that chore to me. An' while I think of it," Topock said casually, "what's the total of them I.O.U.'s you're holdin' on young Tim Ransome?"

"About eighteen hundred dollars—"

"All right. That's plenty—let's have 'em."

There was a visible reluctance in the way Brill got out his billfold, but he passed the papers over

73

without remark and watched Topock button them into his shirt pocket.

Topock looked about with a cold, hard grin. "So Kerwold thinks I wouldn't do much in the cow business, does he?" His laugh was a soft thing, exultant. "Gents, in a month we'll be owning this country."

CHAPTER 9

NIGHT RIDERS

WHAT DUARTE VARGAS had said in Brill's back room concerning Sam Kerwold and the departure of the homesteaders' wagons from Wildcat Hill was not, strictly speaking, true—leastways it was not the whole truth. He had implied that Old Sam had not talked with the wagon men, whereas, as a matter of fact, Kerwold had. With Vargas right at his side, Sam Kerwold had ridden up to the homesteaders' camp. His remarks, though brief, had been courteous and not at all unfriendly. He mentioned admiring their grit and fortitude, flattered their intelligence at picking such good ground, and then, casually, had expressed his surprise at their daring in thinking to file on land so soon to be put up for lease at public auction. "Of course," he said, "the land's open right now to filing, but with all these womenfolks an' kids along, I would think you'd rather pick land that—even though it might not be so good as this—wouldn't be so apt to cloud your horizon with gun-smoke."

The homesteaders eyed him with varying stages of unease.

Old Sam explained. "You see, boys, this here's the way the thing shapes up. Three-four big outfits is after this lease; each one of them, I reckon, is figurin' to bid it in—I understand there's considerable feelin' about it. Fact is, I'd like to bid it in myself, as far as that goes. But you folks are on it and I appreciate your rights. Far as I'm concerned you can stay, an' welcome. But some of these outfits ain't broadminded as I am; they'd call you 'weed-benders' an' figure you got no more right to this land than plain squatters. Some of 'em might get a little rough. Until right lately this country has all been open range—free grass, you understand; anybody's land for the grazin'. Seein' your boys plowin' it up is liable to make some of these fellows pretty ringy. I don't know that they'd actually molest you, but in my time I've seen some pretty ugly things happen to folks that was plowin' up grass."

He paused a bit to let these words sink in a little; and it was plain the wagon men were worried. "I'm not tryin' to dictate to you fellows; I wouldn't undertake to say what you ought to do—that's one of the fine things about this country, a man does what he sees fit to do, the choice is strictly his own. But in your place," Kerwold said, and his tone was a little more somber, "I think I'd hunt me a place with more elbow room, somewheres the cow outfits wasn't quite so big. It's not much pleasure," he went on, "puttin' your life savin's into a place and then have some damn cowman burn you out. Not much fun, either, gettin' up some morning to find your best saddlers hamstrung, your fences cut an' your stock run off or slaughtered. Things like that seem to happen round here and they don't much care who they happen to. My own wire was cut tonight—three miles of it slashed to ribbons an' half the posts lugged off to feed somebody's cook stove.

"Now there's some land over east of here— over by Yellow Jacket Spring; *good* land, too, an' never taken up, and no big cow outfits to bother you. I ain't sayin' you ought to go there, but in your place that's where I'd go. You do whatever you think is best for you—that's the nice part about this country; you got that privilege. Good night."

That was what Sam Kerwold told them and two hours later they were gone. Not toward New River and the rest of the homestead outfits, as Vargas had suggested when relating their departure to Topock, but creaking and clanking eastward toward the Yellow Jacket and Methodist Mountain.

And there was one small other thing that Vargas had forgotten to mention. The sign had been rubbed out, he said—and it had, for two-three miles. But he had not seen fit to tell them he had rubbed the tracks out himself.

When Bufford Dane had said good night to Holly at the back door of the Ransome store building, she quite naturally had supposed that he was going to bed himself; and he did go into the storeroom she had placed at his disposal, but he did not get into the bunk.

He sat down on its edge and pulled his boots off, dropped them noisily on the floor. Rising, then, he picked them up and, carrying them in his left hand, returned soundlessly to the porch. With his weight gingerly settled against the porch edge, he put the boots back on again and, quietly making his way to the stable, hoisted his gear to a shoulder and stealthily led the blue roan away. A quarter of a mile from Ransome's he put the animal under gear, stepped into the saddle and struck off south and east. Others besides Holly Ransome would have been startled had they known this; the thought put its own kind of smile across Dane's dark and wind-whipped cheeks.

Dane's glance went up to the stars. Be several hours till dawn. This country was unfamiliar to him and the moonless night disclosed few land-marks. He rode slowly, not so much confused as cautious. He had no wish to be discovered by chance wayfarers.

He kept an easy pace until, some half hour

later, he cut the trail he had been hunting. This he followed for three miles until certain his sign was lost among the tracks of other travelers. He swung then to the left, putting the blue roan's head dead east.

Near one he reached the footslopes leading up to Wildcat Hill. A gentle walk took him quartering through these rises. When he sighted the first of the wagons he stopped the horse and dismounted. Leading the animals, he inched forward slowly till he'd gotten the lay of things. Then into the saddle he went again; walked the horse grimly into the firelight.

There were startled exclamations, a smothered curse or two. Men came out of their blankets nervously; fire showed the glint of fear in their eyes. That stilled and watchful waiting showed the state of their unease.

Dane said: "Who's the leader of this outfit?"

A man came out of the shadows and stopped across the fire from Dane. He said reluctantly, "I am."

"Guess you understand," Dane said, "you're squattin' on a lease. Got anything to tell me why these wagons shouldn't be burned?"

Back in the shadows a woman gasped. A child started sniveling and was instantly hushed.

The wagon boss said, "That talk won't buy you nothin', mister. We know our rights. This land ain't leased—nor won't be if we file."

"That's right," Dane said, and let the stillness gather. There was in him a strong dislike for this chore, but his indebtedness to Sam Kerwold went back a long, long way. And he was a man who paid his debts.

The man before him shifted weight. He said a little harshly: "What are you here for, then?"

"There's one or two things," Dane said, "you'd better know before you file."

And when the quiet became again intolerable the wagon boss growled, "What are they?"

Dane took his time in answering and his look got wholly bleak. "First and foremost," he said then, "there's this to be considered. The cows are goin' to have this land whether you file on it or not. Past experience should tell you this— if it don't you can take my word for it. This is cattle country. It's goin' to stay cattle country no mater how many nesters get themselves killed, no matter how many wagons have to be burned. Why butt your heads against a damn stone wall? There's plenty good land to the east of here— land you can have an' welcome. But you can't have this . . . Understand me? This land belongs to the cows."

The wagon boss was rattled. Dane's words were having effect. Back in the shadows the child cried again and this time nobody stopped it. The wagon boss was badly placed. Pressure of opinion moved him to get out the makings with what was intended to be an appearance of unconcern. But he couldn't cut it. The shake of his hands spilled tobacco and with a sudden curse he flung the stuff away from him. Defiance edged his sullen stare and brashly, reckless, he snarled:

"All right. You've had your say—now I'll have mine! You damn cow wallopers think you own the earth—"

"Just a minute."

Dane's soft drawl was wholly quiet, yet it stopped the man in mid-sentence, stopped him with his mouth still open—left him that way, stiffly.

Into this quiet came a man's startled gasp. "My God! That's Bufe Telldane!"

They were like a wail, those nerve-jerked words that came from behind the wagon boss. They seemed to sear these homesteaders' minds with the scorch of a branding iron. Color fled their cheeks and panic dropped their jaws. They stood behind their leader like a row of blasted trees, their features blank as pounded metal. The wagon boss's eyes seemed frozen as they stared in glassy fascination at the mounted man before him.

Such was the shocking power that lay in that dread name.

Dane, lounged loosely in the saddle, saw the

consternation in their faces and knew that his work was done. There would be no wagons left on Wildcat Hill by dawn.

He nodded coldly. "Yes. I'm Bufe Telldane. Do you need any further reasons why you had better get off this lease?"

The wagon boss made some attempt at pulling himself together. There was no belligerence left in him now; only a marveling kind of wonder. He seemed surprised to find himself still alive and capable of movement. He said huskily, "No— no, I reckon not. We—we'll get hitched up right away."

Dane nodded silently and backed his horse out of the light, and a few yards off watched patiently till, creaking and clanking, the wagons, got at last into line, rolled wearily off toward the east.

And still he sat there, dismally, loose jointed in the saddle, chin on chest and thoughts gone bleak as any in the homesteaders' minds. He was not proud of this night's work; there was no satisfaction in him. He had achieved the object of his ride, and by that much had lessened Kerwold's hold on him. But he took no pleasure from the performance, nor from contemplation of it. If the fact that the homesteaders' moving had been accomplished without resort to gunplay were any consolation, his face did not reveal it.

He was still there in the saddle when wind brought new smell of dust to his nostrils, and a short time later his keen ears told him a ridden horse was mounting toward the hilltop. Afterwards he saw the rider come quartering out of the night and briefly stop, outlined in the dying embers' glow. He saw the man lean from his horse, watched him study the track-marked ground, and then, still watching, saw him canter across the broad plateau and vanish in the direction the wagons had gone.

He was there, still later, when the man came back, leading his horse and with a jackpine's branch carefully wiping out the trail. The man's face wore a grin when, finally, by the fire he stopped and, satisfied, broke the branch to bits and flung them on the embers. There was a tiny blaze and by that light Dane saw his face.

The man was Kerwold's foreman, Vargas.

CHAPTER 10

"MY GOD—TELLDANE!"

TELLDANE got down when the man had gone.

He stripped the gear from his roan, turned the animal loose on a picket rope and then strode off a ways and there threw his saddle down and, drawing a tarp up over him, put his head upon it and went to sleep.

He slept at once, for this was his will and he had trained himself to the habit. There were those who claimed that he never slept—that a man with his past could not. But these were wrong; he slept, and well; no ghosts could run Telldane's life.

His awakening, like all his acts, was sudden. One moment he lay sleeping, the next he was awake—completely so.

He let no sign betray it. His eyes stayed closed. He had not moved; his breathing continued natural. But all his faculties were alert and functioning. No sound had brought him out of sleep, no touch—nothing a man could lay hold of. Yet Telldane knew there was danger near; it was this sixth sense had roused him.

Something breathed near him and crack-like his closed eyes came open. Just the merest slit. Yet beneath the tarp that look promoted movement. His right hand moved—not quick, not far; but when it stopped it had solid hold of a gun butt.

The moon was up and by its light a figure showed grim-crouched above him. By his head it was. Squatted on its bootheels with blurred face scant inches from Telldane's own.

Telldane's eyes came completely open. His left hand flung the tarp aside, his right hand brought the pistol up—straight up, cocked and leveled, muzzle gaping into the crouched man's face.

"Get back."

With a startled oath the man reared back on his bootheels. Both hands jumped above his hat and a horse, scared squawk spilled out of him. "Don't shoot! Don't—My God! *Telldane!*"

The moments crawled while Telldane watched him grimly. As the seconds passed, the silence thickened. A kind of shake got into the fellow's knees and he blurted with obvious sincerity, "God, Bufe—I hadn't no idear 'twas you. . . ."

"I believe you," Telldane said, and a cold amusement edged his voice. Then the amusement was gone and the voice was only cold—an extreme cold that had unnerved tougher men than this one. "What are you doing here, Holcomb?"

Holcomb winced, but recovered quickly and said with his cheeks wholly bland: "Why, I'm a rancher, Bufe—'member how I was always het up to be one? Well I am one now. Got a pretty fair outfit—Straddle Bug, up near Gone Wrong Canyon."

"You picked a good location," Telldane murmured. Then, more sharply: "But that's not answering my question. Hunkerin' over a sleeping man that way will one day get your face blown off."

"I can see that." Holcomb loosed a gusty breath. "God!"

"What were you up to? 'Fraid you'd miss if you didn't get real close, were you?"

Holcomb's face registered horrified denial. "You know I wouldn't go for to shoot you, Bufe—"

"Not if I saw you startin', you wouldn't. Now quit beatin' about the bush an' say quick what you were up to."

"Why—I—I wa'nt up to nothin', hardly. Honest, Bufe! Why, I ain't got no better friend in the whole wide world'n what you been—"

"Glad to see you appreciate it," Telldane said dryly. "Guess you were out huntin' strays or something—s'pose they're easier caught at night, aren't they?"

Holcomb was not confounded. The shine of sweat was on his face but he said doggedly: "Ha-ha! One of your little jokes, eh, Bufe? Recollect you allus was queer that way. Matter of fact,

I *was* huntin' strays. Some of my fence got cut the other night an'—"

"Never mind improvin' on it." Derision curved Bufe Telldane's lips. Some remembered need then changed their slant abruptly. He said—and his tone was solemn: "I've got one word for you, Ab Holcomb. You can consider this a warning; and there won't be any more of them. You keep out of what's brewing in this basin, or—"

"God's sake, Bufe—"

"Never mind the protestations. An' you can tuck that paraded virtue back in the mothballs with your conscience. There's trouble—*bad* trouble—shaping up in these mountain meadows. See that you keep out of it."

Giving the man no time for jawing, Telldane turned and strode after his horse.

CHAPTER 11

THE BEST LAID PLANS—

FALSE DAWN was shoving its first gray light across the basin when Bufe Telldane rode down from the hills and approached the Ransome store. As a rule, only members of the cow-punching clan were abroad at such ungodly hour. Perhaps this thought had some part in the surprise that was slimming his glance as he eyed intently the three strange broncs loosely tied to the storefront's veranda.

Tossing his own reins over the rail, Telldane got thoughtfully out of the saddle. There was laughter inside and rough talk that he could not distinguish; nor could he make out Holly Ransome's voice—just man sound, and not particularly pleasant. He stood there moveless a moment, undecided. He hitched up his cartridge belt and took a step toward the porch. He recalled then how the porch boards creaked and with a tiny shake of the head he went around the place and entered from the rear.

The kitchen was empty, but voice sound was louder now, drifting back out of the store. He stopped by the door leading through, stood paused there an instant, considering. Something he heard then put a cold sensation along his back. He kicked the door wide open and stepped through with a gun in his hand.

He didn't speak. He didn't need to. The situation was plain all round. Ransome was in a chair and the girl, cheeks putty-white, was against the wall near by him. One man stood with his back to Telldane; he had a pointed gun on the Ransomes and his ribald talk was directed at Holly while his two companions were rifling the safe. The crash of Telldane's boot opening the door had pulled this fellow's head clear round. Before the safe his companions crouched like carven images. They wore no masks and their startled looks betrayed the state of their emotions.

"Drop it," Telldane said, and the man whose weapon had been menacing Holly and her father let go his pistol instantly. It struck the floor with a brittle clatter just as the front door was flung open by Topock who came wickedly in with a gun in each fist.

In that second of switched attention that Telldane's glance wheeled to find Guy Topock there was a crash of breaking glass and Bufe Telldane's back-flashing stare showed the men at the safe going through a window. He slammed one swift shot and was starting forward when the third man dived between Topock's knees and went skidding onto the porch. Telldane's charge was tripped by Topock's foot. Both men went down in a tangle. By the time they had extricated themselves and Telldane had reached the porch, the three erstwhile robbers were aboard their horses and quirting hard up the hillside.

Topock, diving for his horse, blocked Telldane's aim and when the way lay clear again the robbers were beyond good pistol range. With tightening lips Telldane thrust the six-shooter back in his belt and grimly watched while Topock knocked dust from the hill with his rifle. But all three riders crossed the ridge and vanished and Topock, cursing, straightened and slammed the rifle back into its scabbard.

"Of all the rotten luck!" He wheeled abruptly, belligerently. "What the hell was goin' on here anyway?"

Telldane without answering was turning into the store when Topock's arm roughly flung him around. "By God, I asked you somethin', mister! I asked what was goin' on!"

His loud talk brought the Ransomes out. They watched by the door, still shaken, nervous. But Telldane didn't look at them. His glance met Topock's contemptuously. "Askin' *me*, are you?"

"Yes I'm askin' you—an' I'll have an answer!"

"Sure you will, if you want one." Telldane's tone was level, his eyes still scornful. "There wasn't nothing happening, as you'd ought to know. Just a little grandstand play that kind of fizzled."

He smiled as Topock's face abruptly reddened, grew scarlet with rage and hate.

Then Topock was lunging forward, reaching for Telldane's shirt collar, snarling blasphemies and vileness. "You damn cow-flunky! Are you insinuatin'—"

"If the boot fits, pull it on."

Guy Topock swung then, a wild and rageful blow designed to catch Telldane unawares—to smash him reeling from the porch and drop him sprawling in the dust; and it probably would have, had it landed.

But Telldane leaned just then. Leaned forward and came swiftly up inside his guard with a teeth-jarring hook that lifted Topock off his bootheels and set him dizzy against a post. His head rolled loosely and for that second it seemed like he would fall. Then with the roar of a bull his head came up; his right hand slapped his pistol's stock, had the weapon half out of leather when Telldane struck again. The cold fury of that blow exploded against the Texan's ear—against its lobe and the base of his jaw. It drove him stumbling from the porch. He struck the ground off balance and lurched three staggering, uncontrolled steps that caromed him solidly against the tie rail and hung him there by an outflung arm among the snorting horses.

A malicious satisfaction sat the slant of Telldane's cheeks.

Holly looked from him to Topock with a startled wonder on her face, and when her eyes came back a kind of fear was in them; that and something else. The something else took over and she coldly turned and went inside the store.

But old Ransome's eyes were bright and round and the shape of his lips was wholly pleased. His hands were clenched and he kept mumbling over and over something that to Telldane sounded suspiciously unorthodox.

Telldane smiled a little wryly and stood gently rubbing his knuckles. But the bleakness of his stare remained intently, watchfully, on Topock.

The Texan stirred. He pulled the chin up off his chest and rolled bleared eyes about him dazedly. But there was no recognition in his face for what he saw. He was like some shanghaied sailor first awakening at sea. Then change rocked across his face, reshaping it to the malignant pattern of his bestial thoughts.

Dread edged Ransome's gaze as the Texan, groaning, got himself afoot and stood there, swaying groggily. His high roan coloring was gone; the bloated cheeks showed livid, mottled. There was something wild, abysmal, unreasoning, in the look he put on Telldane.

Telldane smiled remotely. "Got enough?"

Topock wheeled then, went lurching to his horse without reply. One shaking hand sought out the horn and he dragged himself into the saddle and rode directly off.

CHAPTER 12

A MAN DECIDES

TELLDANE saw very clearly what the Texan had been up to. Topock *himself* had planned the robbery, had hired those three to play their parts that he might appear in the nick of time to save the Ransomes' money and be deemed by them a hero. But luck had defeated him—the luck that had brought Telldane upon the scene to witness and to blast it. Telldane had guessed the thing was a put-up job the moment Topock came through the door; had been certain of it when the Texan twice had blocked his aim at the departing robbers and then, himself, had missed them. He wondered a little grimly if it had been Topock who had recently tried to bushwhack him. Though he'd said nothing about it, *someone* had tried to get him with a rifle. It was early this morning while he'd been riding to the store— just before he'd come out of the hills while the light was yet uncertain. It had been close the way that lead had viciously banged off the horn of his saddle.

Breakfast was eaten pretty much in silence.

There was little talk, and this was mainly enthusiastic comment from old Ransome on the way Telldane had given 'that tough Texan what he's been asking for.' Holly listened in a scornful silence that soon choked off the old man's talk. He quit the table when he finished eating.

Telldane was amused at the way the girl ignored him. Her frozen courtesy did not bother him in the least. He cared nothing for her opinion—cared no more for what she thought of him than he would for a bullsnake's hissing. Both were harmless, beneath his notice. And he had learned by now that women were all alike. Put a sack over their heads and shake them up and you couldn't tell one from the other.

But he harked to what she was saying. Politeness demanded that.

"I suppose you feel real proud of yourself," she observed with a cold disdain.

The nod his head gave was not for her but for the cherished conviction her tone and manner vindicated. She appeared blithely intent on proving his conception of women a just one. Shallow, empty-headed, selfish. She was like all the rest, he thought—deriving their greatest enjoyment when they were ripping some man to pieces. Oh, Telldane knew them! They liked to pose as demurely innocent while, catlike, trying out their claws. Their chiefest sport was had in discovering and dissecting the varying degrees of passion they were able to rouse in a man. They were like black widow spiders; and he reflected with pitying condescension what great fools were men like Topock who sought to shackle them for parlor ornaments. Why, they'd safer coddle vipers!

He knew a second's regret for having exposed the Texan's hand. The punishment would have been as sure and a deal more fitting had he let the man's ruse succeed.

"Of course," Holly told him scornfully, "your intention was to make me believe that Guy Topock was back of that robbery—that he hired those men to rob us. I hope you realize your time was wasted—"

"Aren't good intentions always?"

"Oh!" she cried. "A philosopher, too!"

"Too?" he said incautiously. "What else am I discovered to be?"

"A drifting bravo, certainly. Gun fighter is stamped all over you!" She said with curling lip: "Are you finding lots of bidders for your guns in Tonto Basin?"

He said a little grimly: "What give you the idea I was huntin' any?"

"Isn't that why you came here?"

His regard for her was reticent. His glance was resentful, hostile. She was like the rest of them—slick with her words; could flap her tongue any way she'd a mind to. There was no use arguing.

No use trying to match them. A man was beat before he started.

Then a perverse humor seized him, a mood quite as contrary as her own. He said maliciously: "Yes, that's so. I picked the right spot for finding trouble. Why, only last night I run them crazy waggoners plumb off the Wildcat Hill—"

"Oh!" she cried, cheeks shading pale; and, holding aside her skirts as she passed him, got out of her chair and hastened off—no doubt to tell her father.

Well, let her tell him—let her tell the whole damn basin. By all means let her tell it! Give those bucks a thing or two to think about. He would like to see Guy Topock's face when the Texan finally heard it.

But he had plenty to think about himself— one thing especially; and his face grimed up as he thought of it. What bitter irony that the cause of his own downfall should be here in person to confound him! He had thought to have done with that, to have put its curse behind him. But three reckless years had not done this; it began to look as though three thousand wouldn't. He could not think of her calmly. The ignominious truth— though he denied it savagely—was that he was still fool enough to care for her. And now to find that she was here—that she was the daughter of old Sam Kerwold who held Bufe in his debt as result of past relations—this was the final straw!

With a muttered oath he crushed his smoke, grinding it bitterly into his plate. All the world must be bent in laughter at the luck of Bufe Telldane. That luck had once been a by-word. It bid fair to be again, he thought, and got wickedly to his feet, all the lines of his face made harsh by the rageful passion that rode him.

What were Kerwold's puny troubles when set beside his own? Why should Bufe Telldane risk his life (not that it was worth much!) and besmirch still further his already tarnished repute to help the father of the person who had spoiled that life in the first place?

By God, he would not!

To hell with them! Kerwold had brewed this range war; let him stew in it! Let him hoard his water—let him grab his land and wire it! Let him fight his own damn battles! It was no skin off Bufe Telldane's nose!

And if Kerwold were licked, were humbled, then serve him right—serve that stuck-up filly of his right also! Maybe it would knock some of the damn pride out of her!

With the thought, Telldane slammed out of his chair. He would get on his horse and ride. Shake the dust of this feuding basin. Jane had made a fool of him once—she would not get that chance again! He'd been a fool, all right, and a soft-headed fool, but he'd not be one any longer!

Ransome called to him as he strode through the

store, but the clack of Bufe's spurs was the only answer the old man got. Telldane was geared to getting out before the soft streak in him changed his mind again.

The mood shoved him round the house and headed him toward the stable. But halfway there he brought up with a snort. The roan was hitched to the rail out front. He retraced his steps, impatiently rounded the porch. Yes, the roan was tied there, head down, dozing. With his hand on the horn Telldane paused, harsh of eye, grim-scowling. Sam, after his fashion, was a fine old man. Be pretty ornery, running out on him this way. Sam was depending on him—had every right to do so. That the obligation had been incurred without Telldane's sanction or approval was neither here nor there; that obligation existed. It was a just one. With every reason for standing pat—with none at all for helping him, Sam Kerwold three years back had saved Bufe's life, and it was Telldane's code that he must repay what the world—had it known—would have regarded as a favor.

Bufe did some thinking, bitterly weighed the pros and cons. But it all came back to that. Kerwold had once risked much to save Bufe's life and Bufe was bound to square it.

Well, it would soon be over, one way or the other. And he needn't spend any time at Kerwold's—in fact, from every standpoint, the farther he stayed from Kerwold's, the better for all concerned. It would not be necessary to see Jane again—no one need know they had ever been acquainted. *He* wouldn't tell; and it was a lead-pipe *cinch* she wouldn't!

Yes, he'd stay a little longer. Till the Flying K was on safe footing; till he'd driven Sam's enemies out of the brush—or killed them. For it would probably come to that. Some way Topock had his knife out for Sam; and someone else, for a long time back, had been whetting up his cleaver. Bufe would take care of these birds, then drift, get out of the country.

Thus resolved, he was turning away from the blue roan's saddle when a bullet's whine drilled past his cheek and rifle's sound smashed challenge from the hills.

CHAPTER 13

DUE WARNING

TOPOCK HAD CLAIMED he didn't trust anyone; yet all his plans were geared to and controlled by information Duarte Vargas had furnished.

Brill carried out his orders and started rumor circulating that Gann was talking sheep again and the word was spread with dispatch. To Holcomb, Brill said that Gann was tanking up these days and threatening to down Ab Holcomb on sight. Holcomb's cheeks got black with anger and he stomped from the place breathing brimstone. When Gann came, Brill mentioned casually that Holcomb was making war talk again, bringing up that forgotten business about his waterholes getting poisoned; and Gann, too, went away snarling oaths and curses. But to make sure the seed was planted on good ground, Topock sent Andy Cooper and his raiders out one moonless night; and next day Holcomb was around with an outraged tale of gutted buildings and hamstrung horses, and Gann's friends heard of pulled down fences and dead, stampeded cattle.

It looked a heap like one more night would see red blood smeared across the moon.

Jesse Brill prepared for trouble.

His precautions were few and simple. He took all the cash from his safe and stuffed it in a money belt which he strapped about his waist. He put his spare socks in his bedroll and with that bulk across his left shoulder, was starting for the door when he remembered the cash in the till. He went and got it, cramming it in his pockets. He took one final look around. He glanced at the clock above the bar—3 p.m. of a hot afternoon; something warned him it would be a lot hotter by this same time tomorrow.

He wheeled and was almost to the door again when it opened and a man came in—a stranger Brill had never seen before. But he knew who it was and that knowledge disturbed him, unsettled him. He took three more steps and stopped, rooted by a sudden fear.

There was nothing of menace in the stranger's pose. But Brill didn't like the smile on his lips— nor the cold, hard light of his stare.

Brill licked dry lips, at a loss to understand himself. Seemed like his blood had turned to water. He'd been hurrying, anxious to get out of this place, to get clear out of the country. Yet here he stood, moveless, speechless, bathed in an icy sweat.

The man by the door seemed to read his

thoughts. The smile on his face grew wider. "Don't let me keep you, Brill. Run right along if you want to."

But Brill did not move. In an agony of fear and indecision he stood there gaping like a ninny. He wanted desperately to go, but something in that yonder man's stare kept him anchored in his tracks. He felt abruptly queer, light headed; the place was hot as Egypt, yet there were cold chills crawling his back.

The stranger quit the door, came catfooting forward a step or two. "Got a pencil, Brill? Got a paper handy?"

"You—" Brill moistened his lips again. "You mean a paper for writin' on?"

"I wasn't figuring to build no kite."

What hell's kind of talk was that? Brill didn't like the fellow's look—it was a sight too cold and watchful. Remindful of a spider with his eyes fixed on a fly.

Unaccountably Brill shivered and a shake got into his legs. He sought to pull himself together. "There's a pencil on the bar," he mumbled; and watched the stranger get it. A faint blur of motion then grabbed the turning tag-end of Brill's gaze, whipped it nervously around. From a corner of the window next the door Llano Tallbook's face stared in at him. *No!*—that sly and malevolent gaze of Pecos Gann's wagon boss went beyond Brill—must be fixed upon the stranger.

Gone stiffly still as a statue, Brill saw jubilation suddenly brighten Tallbook's slitted stare; saw a gun barrel come into sight beside the mask that was Llano's face—saw that cold tube shift and focus.

Gun's thunder shook the room, lashed the walls in shattered echoes. Llano's head fell away from the window with a blue hole through its forehead.

Brill whirled to find the stranger smiling, a smoking pistol in his hand. "Third time's a charm," the stranger drawled, and sheathing his gun, went across to a post and with a knife removed the tacks from a land bid notice and, reversing it, scrawled something on its back with the pencil he had picked up off the bar.

Still rooted, Brill watched him put it back on the post, drive the tacks in with his gun butt. "Guess that'll do," he nodded, and with a hard look at Brill, went out.

Mechanically Brill walked up to the post. He stood there for a long time whitely eying the man's scrawled message. He braced himself against the post, went out of the place like a man gone blind.

Hours later Guy Topock came in. He stared around impatiently, several times shouting for Brill. He went behind the bar then and, thoughtfully, looked in the till. He scowled at the open safe, deep-frowning, finally helped himself from a bottle. He was lifting his glass when he saw the handwriting tacked to the post and crossed as Brill had crossed to stand and stare—but unlike Brill—very briefly.

"My God!" he said, and the glass fell out of his hand.

Completely absorbed he read again:

TO WHOM IT MAY CONCERN
By this writing due warning is served on all and sundry that homesteaders, nesters or anyone else caught squatting on the Wildcat lease lands will be personally and speedily taken care of by
Yours truly,
BUFE TELLDANE.

With a curse, Topock ripped the warning from the post and tore it into bits. Still swearing, and with a face gone black as thunder, he went out of Brill's at a wicked lope, flung himself into the saddle and an instant later was racking across the valley, spilling blasphemies at every jolt.

CHAPTER 14

AT HOLCOMB'S

AROUND EIGHT o'clock of a bright crisp morning two days later, Telldane rode down out of the pines and into Ab Holcomb's ranch headquarters. He had been doing a pile of thinking. What was going on was obvious enough; how to prevent its continuing was the thing that most was bothering him. It wasn't so much Kerwold's lack of popularity among his neighbors that was bringing this trouble to Flying K, as it was some older, deeper rooted score. Someone wanted Flying K range or wanted Sam Kerwold smashed. It was the only reasonable explanation for what was building in this basin. *Why* was another matter; Telldane was not concerned with motives—not primarily, at least. His interest lay in blocking the things; in stopping it, thus easing himself out of Kerwold's debt that he might be free to ride.

He saw the man by the saddle shed door— saw the rifle the man had hold of. But, ignoring them both, he stepped to the porch and knocked. Holcomb's heavy voice came at once the length of a hallway. "Gettin' goddam polite these days! Come in."

He found the Straddle Bug boss in an office at the back of the house. Holcomb's quick, upwheeling stare was one of surprise, Bufe thought; and of something else—concern, maybe.

But the man had his wits about him. He said rumblingly: "Howdy, Bufe—been wonderin' when you'd drop around. Mindful of ol' times, ain't it—me an' you gettin' together this way. Sit down. What's under your hat?"

Telldane took off the hat and looked.

Holcomb forced another grin. "Same ol' Bufe." He said sententiously: "Nothin' ever changes, does it?"

"I been wonderin'," Telldane mentioned, and with a grim look peeled the gloves from his hands and laid them on the desk. "What do you know about Brill's killing?"

Holcomb looked nervous. He said vehemently: " 'Fore God, Bufe, I had no hand in that!"

Sweat broke out on his forehead. He shifted under Telldane's stare; pounded the desk in protest. "Goddamit, I wasn't even *near* the place!"

Telldane kept on looking at him.

Holcomb found the silence disturbing. He snarled: "Why pick on *me* ever' time somethin' happens? You run me out of Texas—you goin' to run me out of this place, too?"

"Depends," Bufe said. "What you got against Pecos Gann?"

"Gann!" Holcomb hauled his boots down off the desk angrily. "Who said—"

"It's common talk. What's back of it?"

"Ain't anything back of it. It's a damn malicious lie! Dammit, all I *get* is trouble," he snarled resentfully. "Ain't nobody got a good word for me!"

"Kerwold ain't turned against you, has he?"

"What's the meanin' of that?"

"Gave you a start in the cow business, didn't he?"

With a bitter oath Holcomb surged from his chair.

"Sit down," Telldane said. "I ain't finished. The story's goin' round that you and Gann had trouble over sheep. That Gann came to you with a proposition; that you turned it down flat—said you'd kill every sheep he brought in. It was right after that someone burned his range. And then your waterholes was poisoned . . ."

Telldane stopped at the look on Ab's wide face. "What's the matter? Ain't that so?"

Holcomb was eying him queerly. "Some of it's so, I guess—the part about the fire an' poisoned waterholes. But you sure as hell got your signals mixed. It was Pring—Gus Pring—Gann put that sheep deal up to. Knew better'n to try that game on me. After Pring turned him down, he

108

come over here with another bee in his bonnet—Gann, I'm talkin' of. Wanted to throw his spread an' mine together, wanted to start a syndicate—declared we could grab this country—run the rest of 'em outa business." He added virtuously: "I told him no—nothin' doin'. I didn't want no part in it."

"Why's he threatening to gun you?"

"That squirt! Gun *me?* I could shoot the buttons off his pants any day he names!" The look Holcomb shoved at Telldane now was blackly edged with suspicion. "Where'd you get that anyway?"

Telldane shrugged. "Then it isn't true?"

"It may be true, but it's goddam cockeyed if it is! Gann might be wantin' like hell to see me planted—never was no love lost between us—but it sure ain't like him to go throwin' his jaw around that way. Somebody must be shovin' him."

The same thought had just struck Telldane. "Know who it would be?"

Holcomb shook his head. "He's seein' a lot of that new guy, Topock—leastways I've heard he is."

Telldane considered. "You think, then, someone's tryin' to set you two at each other's throats?"

"What else *can* I think?" Holcomb growled irritably: "There's somethin' goin' on round here that I ain't in on. Somethin' big! Cattle's bein' rustled wholesale—"

"You wouldn't know anything about *that,* of course." Telldane's grin flushed Holcomb darkly; brought him cursing from the chair to tower above Bufe, cocked and wicked.

Without alarm Telldane glanced up at the stocky man amusedly. "What's the matter, Ab? Conscience botherin' you?"

"I've had enough of your gab," Holcomb said, and his face was ugly. "I told you once I've quit all that. I'm goin' straight these days—you hear me? I'm a respectable rancher now an'—"

"Sure, sure," Telldane agreed; "you're a changed man, Ab—I can see it." He said soothingly, "Kerwold's been your friend, ain't he? Well, Sam's in trouble now—bad trouble; an' it might be you could help him."

Holcomb pondered that; eased off. "You workin' for Sam?"

"Sam did me a favor once. I'm tryin' to repay it. Thought mebbe you'd be wantin' to help Sam, too—"

"Would if I could—"

"Might be you can. You didn't drop Brill, did you?"

Holcomb jerked back like a man slapped across the face. His cheeks went darkly ruddy and he was lifting clenched fists when Bufe said coolly:

"There, there; I was only askin'. *Somebody*

killed him. You never set fire to Gann's range—never tried any tricks with Gann's cattle?"

Holcomb said darkly: "No!"

"An' you don't think he poisoned your water-holes, set fire to your line camps or hamstrung those horses?"

"What's all that got to do with Kerwold?"

"I don't know. I'm tryin' to figure who's back of this. You don't think it's Gann, eh?"

"Know damn well it ain't—you could shake Gann's brains in a thimble an' never make ary a rattle. Look here—" growled Holcomb, abruptly, frankly. "You can put that in the book. I ought to know. Guy you're talkin' about's Gann Holcomb—my brother."

Telldane whistled.

"Surprises you, eh? Well, that ain't a patch to the surprise I got when I heard he was braggin' to gun me! I tell you, boy, there's somebody bigger'n him back of this—somebody *really* big—somebody that's got a think-box that would make yours an' mine look puny. Who is it? What's he after?"

"That," Telldane nodded, "is what I'm tryin' to find out."

"Well, you won't find out from me. *I* don't know." Holcomb scowled about him irritably. "It's sure got *me* beat!"

"Who was it you were expectin' when you hollered for me to come in?"

Holcomb's look had been frank, had been keyed to a patent sincerity. But suddenly his eyes showed watchful and his roan cheeks were subtly altering to their sly, remembered slanting. All the lines of his face showed change and he said wonderingly: "Why—why, nobody, Bufe—I wasn't expectin' nobody—"

Boot sound, that moment striking echoes from the porch, came to interrupt him and a man's hail gave his words the lie. "You in there, Ab? I come over quick as I could, but—"

The voice, like its owner, stopped on the threshold.

Telldane grinned. "Come in, Pring. Never mind the apologies—better late than never, Ab always says."

CHAPTER 15

RIP TIDE

SAM KERWOLD was leaving the harness shed when the Flying K range boss stopped him at the door. "Guess Pring'll be sloshin' his hat on slanchways again, now Miz Jane's back home to roost fer a spell . . ."

At that point something in Kerwold's look stopped Vargas's flow of words. Quickened breathing stirred his chest and the hands that had swung at his sides came gingerly up to rest by hooked thumbs from his gun belt. He said apologetically: " 'Course you're right. It ain't no skin off my nose. But a man can't keep from wonderin' hardly, an' all hands know Gus used to be thicker'n splatters round this outfit—over here sittin' the bag 'bout every other night. 'Course, I know he never had no more chance'n a stumptail bull at fly time, but—"

A dark flush worried Kerwold's cheeks and he said harshly: "What the hell are you gettin' at, Vargas?"

The range boss moved the hands from his gun belt, spread them in a deprecatory gesture. "Well,

I ain't aimin' to be mindin' the other man's personal business, an' of course I don't rightly know how—"

"Never mind whittlin' all the bark off it. If you got somethin' to say, get it said an' done with."

Vargas rubbed the mole on his chin; looked off across the range for a bit. Bringing his glance at last back to Kerwold, he said uneasily, "I just been kind of wonderin', Sam, if you've heard— if you've heard about the way Gus is borrowin' money—"

"Borrowin'? Who from?"

"Well, I don't rightly know. That partic'lar wa'n't included in the rumor I got hold of. Point is what he's borrowin' it *for.*" He stopped and looked at Kerwold brightly. "Like I said, he ain't been round much in the last three years, but now Jane's back from school again I note he's comin' over reg'lar—"

"By the everlastin'!" Kerwold swore. "Get to the point, man, if you got one!"

"We-ell—" Vargas scowled off across the yard. "I don't know's you're goin' to like this, Sam. But from what I hear, he's borrowin' heavy— borrowin', I been told, to bid in that Wildcat lease—"

Sam Kerwold's grip fastened hard on his shoulders. The old man's pale blue eyes were blazing. "You damn pup!" he stormed. "You mean to stan' there an' tell me Gus Pring—the best friend I ever had—is goin' behind my back to take that bid away from me! *Do you?*"

Vargas winced. He raised a warning hand. "Now wait a minute, Sam," he began, but Kerwold cut in savagely.

"Wait, *hell!*" he shouted. "You answer me yes or no, by Gawd! Now *do* you?"

"Well, all I know is . . . If you must—Damn it, Sam! I hate like hell to tell you this, but the answer's *yes*—"

"Where'd you hear this?"

"Got it from that new fella, Topock—"

"Where'd he get it?"

"Says he got it straight from Flimpkin, cashier of that new bank at Globe—"

Kerwold grabbed a rope down from a wall peg, shoved Vargas out of his path and started hotfoot for the horse corral.

"Here—wait!" called Vargas. "Where the hell you goin', Sam?"

Kerwold made no answer. He yanked the corral gate open violently; swung and missed and swung again. Twelve seconds later he was in the saddle, ripping up dust on the trail to Pring's.

It would have been hard to say which showed the greater consternation—Holcomb or Gustave Pring. But Pring's was for that second only. He came with a cool smile into the room. "Hello.

115

Aren't you the gent I met at Kerwold's?—fellow Sam was calling 'Dane'?"

Telldane's glance came abruptly vigilant. He sensed hidden things in the way Pring put that. He said, hardly smiling, "It ain't my name, but that's what I called myself. I'm Bufe Telldane—from Texas."

"Yes," Pring nodded. "I thought so. Remembered seein' your face on a dodger. Sam know who you are?"

"I haven't mentioned it to him."

"Notice you weren't at all bashful about slappin' it on that warning you stuck up at Brill's the other day. What were you tryin' to do there anyway—scare somebody? Sam put you up to that?"

Telldane's opinion of Pring underwent change. The man was sharp as a razor. He wondered what else Pring guessed. But instead of answering, Bufe just smiled.

The boss of Double Bar Circle was a broad-cheeked man, thick lipped and heavy featured. He had skin burnt dark as old leather and a hard, tough way with his eyes; they were odd eyes, palely yellow, lambent and confident—arrogant. He'd a chunky, blocklike figure and hair that was oily and black; it tufted the backs of his fingers and showed from the open neck of his shirt, which was neatly gabardine and tan, matching well the burnt roan of his features.

"It's interestin'," Telldane said, "knowin' what people think of you." He fished out the makings. "Anything else you've noticed?"

Pring's cheeks were bland. "I've *heard* you're some kind of special ranger sent in here by the Governor—but of course I don't believe that. Ain't hardly likely, considering all the money Texas spent various times tryin' to apprehend you. I suppose you've cleared out of Texas for good?"

"You mean for the good of Texas?"

Pring smiled with his lips. "Got a sense of humor, eh? You're to be congratulated. You're the first outlaw I ever met that hand."

"Your acquaintance with outlaws extensive?"

Pring's chuckle was a homey sound, quite comfortably carefree, easy. "As a matter of fact, you're the first one I've met—odd how a man'll say things that way. Are you the man we vote a medal for getting rid of Brill?"

"Afraid I can't claim that honor," Bufe said, and revised his estimation of the Double Bar Circle boss again. It had been a long time since anyone had slung such talk at Bufe Telldane; and while it warned him, it amused him also. He scratched a match on his Levi's and lit the quirley he'd rolled. He lounged back in his chair, puffed contentedly. "Haven't seen Safford lately, have you?"

Pring shook his head. "I've too much to do to keep—"

"For a busy man," Bufe drawled, "I'd say you were pretty well informed. You knew about that warning I tacked up, yet only two men read it—Brill an' that Texan, Guy Topock. And Topock tore it up."

Pring's eyes showed a little narrow. He shrugged. "Things like that get around, Telldane."

Telldane said: "Evidently."

Ab Holcomb stared at them, scowling. "Crissakes! Talk American, can't you?"

But neither man so much as looked at him. Their looks were for each other; watchful, guarded, coolly smiling; they reminded Holcomb of a couple of beef contractors visiting the Indian Agent. They were that coldly civil, that blandly polite. Yet all the while danger's feel kept tightening. The riptide of unshown emotions wiped cold chills across his spine.

"Have you decided," Pring asked, "to take that job I offered?"

Telldane's teeth gleamed a smile of sorts. "I guess not—"

"I could raise—"

" 'Fraid not. Don't believe you could borrow enough."

A frown got tangled in Pring's yellow eyes and he said, voice nettled: "Are you ins—"

"I mean," Telldane grinned coldly, "you couldn't corral money enough. My guns are not for hire."

A contemptuous grunt came out of Pring. "That's crazy! Every man's got a price—"

"That may be your philosophy . . ." Telldane stopped with head cocked—listening. Horse sound came and stopped at the porch. Boots struck gravel, crossed the porch, came echoing down the hall.

Sam Kerwold grimly entered the room and his raking stare found Pring.

CHAPTER 16

GUS PRING

TOPOCK had no need to talk with old Ransome to know whose the hand that had driven Cooper's homesteaders off Wildcat Hill. He knew the moment he saw Bufe's notice. And he remembered where he had seen Bufe before—the man had been pointed out to him as Bufe Telldane that day in Roaring Fork when he had killed Dave Ruddabaugh.

A lot of things came clear to him then and he shivered as he remembered how twice he'd grabbed that gun fighter's shoulder and roughly hauled him round. It was God's own mercy the man hadn't killed him!

But Topock's marveling at this miracle was brief. Where another man—one less bold or less reckless—might have considered it as a 'stitch in time,' Topock's principal reaction as he considered the mauling he had got at Telldane's hands was one of vengeful animosity. His hatred for the gun fighter mounted, and instead of considering ways of avoiding future conflict with the man, Topock's time for the next several hours was taken up with schemes for Telldane's undoing.

It did not prove a fruitful labor.

Still bitterly, wholly malevolent, he turned his attention to ways for keeping Kerwold from getting his hooks on the Wildcat lease lands. Apparently that damned Telldane was working for Flying K—else why had the gun fighter made it his business to put Cooper's homesteaders off? He would have to reckon with Telldane; and he must reckon, too, with Cooper's notion that Sam Kerwold might attempt to lease from the squatters should they succeed in taking over the Wildcat lands. But *that* could be attended later. Right now it was urgent to remove those lands from public auction. There was one way that he could do it, and he grinned when the idea came to him. They'd slipped up on a bet that first time, but they wouldn't be slipping up this time. His black eyes glinted as he told Cooper what to do.

Kerwold's stare was bitter and angry. Without regard for the others, he said without preliminary: "You been borrowin' money, Gus?"

Pring's beefy cheeks got a little flushed. "Reckon I have. Nothing wrong with—"

"Borrow it from that bank at Globe?"

"Really, Sam, I don't see—"

"You don't need to!" Kerwold snapped. "All I want from you is a fair an' square answer—yes or no! Did you borrow with the idea of biddin' in that Wildcat lease?"

Kerwold's look was black and violent, but Gus Pring's gaze was cool, unflustered. He seemed quite at ease; a little puzzled certainly, but entirely free from shame or anxiety. He was much the coolest man in the room. His eyes showed the grave amusement with which some tolerant elder might have regarded a frantic child. He said smoothly:

"Hold on now, Sam; you're all afrother. 'F it comes to that, don't know as I much blame you. Where did you get this wild tale? From Flimpkin, at the bank?"

"Never mind where I got it," scowled Kerwold, the heady anger still traveling his cheeks. "All I want from you's an answer. Straight from the shoulder—yes or no?"

"Tut, tut! Of course the story's not true—I'm a little surprised you'd swallow such stuff. I suppose, in a way, though, the fault's really mine. I did borrow a bit the other day, and from Flimpkin at the First National. Got a few improvements about the place," he mentioned smoothly, "that I've been intending to get busy on. 'Course, I knew well enough the bank would never lend money on—Well, the upshot was, I told Joe Flimpkin I was after the Wildcat lease an' he gave me the money."

Kerwold, under Pring's reproving look, showed

a little sheepish. He cleared his throat two or three times embarrassedly; brought out his pipe, peered in its half-filled bowl and searched his pockets for a match. Pring handed him one, faintly smiling.

Old Sam puffed a moment, plainly without enthusiasm. Taking the pipe from his mouth, red-cheeked, uneasy, he said flustered: "Expect I've not done you much justice, Gus—suspicionin' you the way I been. But hearin' that yarn sudden like I done, kind of knocked me off my feed, I reckon." Backing up came hard to Kerwold, and Pring said, coming to his rescue:

"That's all right. Any buy's liable to cut his stick short when a man starts peddlin' loads of that kind." He said, eyes narrowing, "What I'd like to know is who brought up that bill of goods—"

"Seems like," Telldane drawled, interrupting, "you've forgot what brought you over here so early."

Pring, to whom the remark was addressed, affected not to notice. Still eying Kerwold, he said insistently: "Who was ladling that stuff, Sam?"

But Kerwold shook his head. "Best leave sleepin' dogs alone," he mumbled; and turned to look at Telldane as though only now realizing the stranger's presence. "What was that you was sayin', Dane?"

Telldane shrugged. "I was just commentin' on the tearin' rush with which brother Gus got off his horse this mornin'. Seemed like somethin' was botherin' him—mebbe it was findin' me here ahead of him."

Pring's hard, upwheeling stare was edged with anger, but his heavy lids concealed it quickly and some noted need adjusted his cheeks to an easy, jovial slanting. "No," he declared, "the strutting antics of casual gun fighters have never managed to bother me much. But I have got news—it'll interest all of you—Mister *Dane-Telldane* particularly. There's a new batch of wagons on Wildcat this morning and"—looking regretfully at Kerwold—"I'm afraid they're here to stay."

Kerwold wheeled sharply.

Pring met his look with a shake of the head. "There's a fellow named Willow Creek Wally sort of bossing the outfit—maybe our friend, *Mister Dane* here, knows him—I'd say they might be lodge brothers. At all events, this Wally hombre took pains to tell me they've filed; that trespassers won't be welcome."

Ab Holcomb cursed. Kerwold's cheeks got darkly mottled.

Holcomb snarled explosively: "I fired that goddam range tramp once—thought he'd left the country! By—"

"Gus," asked Kerwold bitterly, "d'you s'pose he's tellin' it straight?"

"About filing?" The Double Bar Circle boss shrugged. "I see no reason to doubt it. Usually speaking, the word of fellows like this Wally ain't worth the amount of breath wasted; but in this instance I'm inclined to think the man's telling the truth. Easy enough to check—"

"No need of that," murmured Telldane. "I'll take care of these squatters."

Pring sneered. "Like you did that first batch? I'm afraid—"

"You needn't be. They'll be on their way before sundown."

"Oh—I see. That notice," Pring said. "Guess you feel it's your bounden duty—"

"We gun fighters," Telldane drawled, "don't worry overmuch about duty. We're like some ranchers that way—obligations never weigh us down."

Pring's cheeks roaned up with anger. He said quickly, unthinkingly: "If that slap was aimed at me—"

Telldane grinned. "What's the matter? Conscience botherin' you? Tut, tut! Don't let it, Gus—'every man has his price.'"

The Double Bar Circle boss, abruptly remembering Kerwold, got a hold on his temper. He said stiffly: "I've no time to waste on riddles. If you're ridin', Sam, I'll go along with you."

Kerwold seemed not in any great hurry. His look was questioningly on Telldane. But Gus Pring had a way about him and that way took the old man out to his horse.

125

CHAPTER 17

A MAN MUST FIGHT

THE sun was high in the afternoon sky when Bufe Telldane came in sight of the camp.

The wagons were there, all right. Drawn up in a circle, their formation a plain hint of expected trouble. They were not the wagons he'd sent rolling east; nor were these the men he had sent east with them.

A different outfit, this; one used to trouble—geared for it. With but two exceptions, all the men of that cocked group were strangers. Hard eyed, features immobile as masks hacked out of wood. The exceptions were Pecos Gann and young Tim Ransome—these Bufe had met that first night at the store.

Riding up to them, he stopped the roan, lazily curling a knee around the horn. He nodded curtly. "Howdy, Ransome. How come you're spendin' time with these gophers?"

Young Ransome scowled, his stare gone sullen.

Gann said belligerently: " 'Cause he's wantin' his rightful share of this basin—same's the rest of us. Any objections?"

Telldane's frosty eyes looked him over. "I can think of some—from his angle. Lost all interest in your health, kid?"

A flush stained the down on Ransome's cheeks.

"You're travelin' with the wrong crowd," Telldane warned him. "Better—"

"Don't let that bastard scare you, Tim," sneered Gann, eying Telldane toughly. "Best thing he does is run sandys. That's Bufe Telldane—name the old women in Texas use to scare their brats with. Ain't nawthin' about him noways for a growed man to be afeared of."

Telldane smiled amusedly. "Much obliged for the introduction. Now that the pleasantries have been attended to, I'd admire to know which one of you wolves is roddin' this outfit."

"I am."

It was a gaunt man said it—a slat-built fellow in bullhide chaps.

Hired-gun hombre was stamped all over him; in the crouch of his body, in the slitted stare—in the long-fingered flexing of his hands. Telldane's glance was edged with derision. "An' who are you?"

"Willow Creek Wally's my handle."

"All right, Willow Creek. Hitch up them wagons an' roll."

The gun fighter's eyes showed a rush of temper. "Like hell!" He said loudly: "Who's figgerin' to make me?"

"The law would make you, I reckon—if I cared to wait that long. Since I don't, I expect likely I can make out to take care of the evacuation myself—"

"You can shout, too!" Gann snarled, cursing. "This here is all government land we're on! It's open to filin'—"

Telldane's teeth showed a cold white smile. "It was," he corrected gently.

Willow Creek Wally said: "That's right—it was. It ain't any more because we've filed on it."

"Someone around here needs glasses," Bufe drawled. "An' the someone ain't me. If you've filed on this strip, you've been wastin' your time—been plumb careless, too, I guess likely. I filed on this land three days ago. At that time, as Gann says, it was government property. But it ain't any more. It's mine. You might not have heard about it, but I posted a notice to that effect at Brill's right after I filed it. You're on the wrong foot, Mister. Hitch up an' roll."

"I guess not," Willow Creek said flatly. "We'll stick around a spell till—"

"Be a longer spell than you're bargainin' for."

A sulky brilliance got in Willow Creek's eyes and the hand that was by his holster spraddled.

"Better not," Bufe said; and some way all the hot color washed out of Willow Creek's cheeks. He stood a moment that way, uncertain; then with a shrug and a sneer he wheeled away and, with

128

a curt command for the others, went angling off toward the horses being held between stretched ropes.

"Well, by God! *Yellow!*" Gann cried; and with a tight-snapped oath wheeled round to Telldane; shook a fist at him, eyes bright with violence. "By grab, you ain't runnin' *me* out, hombre! Not by a jugful! I—"

"You'll be well-advised," Telldane cut in "—unless you're cravin' what Brill asked for—to hitch up your team and get out."

Telldane's words, crystal clear, stopped every man in his tracks. He had an instant's regret for the impulse that had made him drag Brill into this. He had not shot Brill—had not tangled with him—and it was a mistaken strategy, he realized now, to have intimated that he had. These men were probably friends of Brill's. Wild exultation suddenly brightened Willow Creek's eyes. Telldane had precipitated—was swiftly bringing on—the very violence his words had been intended to avoid.

Gann's face was bloated, livid. Bufe saw how his muscles leaped and stiffened; saw the lantern jaw with its cud-bulged cheek jump forward.

He said: "Watch it, Gann!" and set himself there solidly, with all his taut nerves screaming.

Gann may not have ranked high in the annals of fast gun throwing, but Telldane, aboard a horse, was at a considerable disadvantage; and the glitter of his smoky stare showed Gann to be aware of this. Cheeks shaped to lines of cunning, a taunting grin curved the sheepman's mouth. "Your talk is bigger'n Moses," he sneered, "but you're like all the rest of these gun slappers! Noiser'n hell on cart wheels, but—"

Gann's talk abruptly quit. He went back a step still crouched but with his eyes pin-pointed, frantic, a corner of his mouth a-quiver, clawed hand spread above gun butt.

"Go on if you must," Telldane said. "Pull it."

But all Gann's courage had melted. He could feel it leaking out of him, shriveled in the blaze of Bufe's wanton stare. The murderous impulse that had shoved him into this—even the believed advantage that had been his, was gone . . . washed away by the easy confidence of Telldane's posture. Gann would no more have touched his pistol now than he'd have stooped to pat a rattlesnake. He could not think—much less have moved—could only crouch there, frantic, paralyzed; rooted by the knowledge that to draw would be to die.

"Well, do *something,*" Telldane snapped impatiently. "Drag your iron or drag your freight."

But still Gann did not move—he *could* not.

A moment longer Telldane waited. A mirthless laugh came out of him then. With a shrug he kneed the roan around.

That laugh, or that movement, broke the spell.

Wild rage in his face Gann grabbed for his gun. Willow Creek's eyes streaked a warning but Gann was beyond the reach of caution. Humiliated, boiling with anger and hatred, Gann's white-clamped fist jerked the gun from leather—but the back he'd aimed to salivate was no longer pointed toward him. The big roan horse had wheeled clear around and Bufe Telldane was facing him.

Too late Gann saw he'd been neatly tricked—saw the gaping muzzle of Telldane's pistol. His own rising weapon was not quite level when Telldane's roared—just once.

Gann's squat, crouched body jerked and buckeled, a reeling stagger spilled him into the dust where he lay outsprawled, face down, unmoving.

"Jeez!" Tim Ransome's eyes were round.

Telldane drawled: "Any more drygulchers huntin' action?"

In that brittle silence no man moved. No man dared hardly loose a breath.

Telldane grinned at them, coldly mocking.

"Get hitched up an' drag it out of here—*an' don't come back.*" His glance swung then in a slow half circle, seeming to memorize each touched face. It stopped with impact on the frozen pallor of Willow Creek's cheeks. "Tell Guy Topock I'm comin' after him—that he had better move fast if he expects to get clear."

CHAPTER 18

CATTLE BY NIGHT

RIDING back to the store at Ransome's Crossing, Telldane felt no regret for having killed Gann. The man had asked for what he got, and got exactly what his cowardly try had merited. Telldane, conscious only of a grim distaste for the entire business, shoved the man from his mind. He must keep alert, for by this shooting—and the proclamation that had brought it on—he had openly aligned himself with Flying K, and all the forces of wrath and greed and vengeance that were out to down Sam Kerwold would be focused on him. He had taken his stand and must abide by it. There was no retreating possible now. Constant vigilance must be the price he paid for life.

He rode with his Winchester across his lap and with keen eyes searching the brushy slopes, seeking out each covert—probing it, alert for the gleam of gun metal.

But with all this care his mind was not idle. It was a time for thought, and Bufe thought hard. He thought of the things Ab Holcomb had told him—even more about those Ab had left unsaid. And the controlled, masklike countenance of the Double Bar Circle boss frequently flashed across his mind. What hidden thoughts and desires lay behind the man's suave and inscrutable features? What deep purposes and dark intentions lurked behind Pring's lambent stare? He felt no trust of Pring and pondered long the scarce-veiled belligerence of the man's remarks. Plainly Pring was convinced Bufe was backing Kerwold—but could that be a cause for hostility? According to rumor, years back Pring had owed his start here to the same generous hand that had backed Ab Holcomb; Sam Kerwold had advanced the cash and cattle to which the man's present standing was due. Too, Telldane had heard that Pring was a candidate for the prominence to be accorded Kerwold's son-in-law. Pring had every reason, Telldane thought, to be backing Kerwold in this trouble that was brewing—had every reason, yet Bufe was far from satisfied that he was. And Holcomb—which side was Holcomb favoring? Sam's? Or the side of Sam's enemies?

That Sam had enemies aplenty was quite apparent. Topock, of course—and Cooper (Bufe had heard report of their embarrassing expedition to seek Sam's backing). But this trouble went beyond that—had been brewing for months before their coming. That old framed business of Gann and Holcomb was proof enough of this.

What man or group in this basin could have thought to profit by a feud between them? And this guy, Willow Creek, whom Holcomb had last year kicked off the Straddle Bug—where did *he* fit into this? And Vargas? Telldane had not forgot how Kerwold's foreman had met him on the night of his arrival. Sam seemed sure of the man, of his loyalty and straightness. But Telldane was not sure at all. What had the man been doing in those trees that night? For whom had Vargas been waiting? Not for Bufe, certainly, because even had he knowledge of Telldane's coming, he could not have known which trail the man would take.

Who had cold-bloodedly murdered Brill upon the trail to Payson? And why? Why and who had murdered the old Dutch homesteader, Juke Ronstadt? And where was Safford? Was he doing anything to clear these mysteries up? From his words in the store that night, Bufe thought it highly probable that Lou Safford was aiming to throw his weight on the side of Sam's enemies. If this surmise were right, there was a pretty fair chance the marshal was crooked—not that everyone opposed to Flying K was bound to be, but because Guy Topock and his sidekick, Cooper—who were heading at least one flank of the opposition—were pretty obviously crooks and the marshal had appeared to be on first-rate terms with them.

Then there was that business of the stuck-up stage which had taxed Sam Kerwold's pocketbook a couple thousand dollars he could ill afford to lose.

All in all, it looked like the Tonto country was in for a stretch of squally weather.

Pring had said there was a rumor loose to the effect that Bufe was a special ranger sent in here by the Governor. If there was, it was the first that Bufe had heard of it. He could almost wish he *were* a ranger; his work would be so much simpler if he had a badge to back him—simpler, at least, so far as questions and answers were concerned. With a badge he could have cleared up some of these mysteries in pretty short order. But thought of the badge curled his lips derisively. It had been many a day since Bufe Telldane had packed a lawman's tin.

The thought turned his mind back on Kerwold—on the cause of his indebtedness to the grizzled boss of Flying K. Three years ago in Texas—three years almost to the night. He remembered the circumstances well—the Orient Hotel in Pecos—that smoke-fogged barroom with its swinging lamps, the shouts and curses and . . . the sudden silence. He had been a stock detective then—three months on the trail of the McChandless gang and that night was to have furnished the final bit of evidence, the clinching proof that was to make his case complete. But somewhere along the line someone had talked. He was to have met Bob Brady, a ranger, in the bar that night and, together, grab the three McChandless boys and as many of the gang as they could manage. But Brady hadn't come and the McChandless boys were warned. Dode McChandless had stepped up to him as soon as he'd entered the bar. There'd been quick words, a blow. The din of bedlam filled the place as vengeful hands grabbed sixguns. Bufe hadn't had a chance—had been jammed against a wall with Dode McChandless's pistol toughly shoved against his belly, when Sam Kerwold, an utter stranger, had stepped through the lobby door. Bufe still thrilled to the remembered sound of Old Sam's voice dryly saying: "I guess the game is up, boys. Unless you gents are cravin' harps an' halos, don't so much as bat a eyelash. Jest hi'st them dewclaws an' grab for the rafters, an' what I mean—*grab quick!*"

Three years . . . It didn't seem so long.

Bufe sighed. 'Drag' Telldane they'd called him then, and the name had been a by-word, a scourge to long-loop hombres.

Bufe felt suddenly tired and old. The weight of all those yesterdays lay heavy on him now; their turbulence had gutted him, he was just a husk of the man who had made the victory of San Juan Hill that thing of glory the history books named it. Just the husk—the burnt-out husk; a man whose name today was steeped in calumny, anathema—a thing, as Gann had said, to scare bad children with.

Well, he had had his fun he supposed—most folks would say he had. He would lick this thing for Sam if he could and ride on over the hump. Somewhere, some place and time, perhaps, he would find the peace he craved; an end to all this turbulence. Some old, forgotten backwash where the name 'Telldane' had not been heard—where the man could unbuckle his gun belt.

But he must square his debt with Kerwold first . . .

The thought brought another sigh. So many loose ends were cluttering this; there was nothing for a man to bite down on. Stray threads, yes—God knew there were plenty of those! But try to catch one—ravel it; you found it torn from its moorings, laying useless in your hand. Take Guy Topock for example. *He* was that way—a thread in point. He was mixed up in this, certainly—so was Holcomb, Pring, Duarte Vargas. So was Safford, seemed like. But *how?* Yes, that was it! What part were these fellows playing?

There was this rustling business, the original cause of Sam's letter. He believed he understood who was back of these wholesale cattle thefts. That had been Ab Holcomb's trade in Texas, and despite Ab's protestations, he saw no reason for believing the man had changed. And yet—

he had always thought Ab grateful—a man who remembered favors. Certainly Sam's backing him to a new start here should come under that category.

Could it be . . .

The thought snapped off, Telldane going tense before the remembered need for vigilance. His cat-quick glance raked the surrounding shadows with a probing care. Dusk had gathered during his thinking and some way his horse had gotten off the trail.

He sat bolt upright in the saddle attempting to orient himself—striving to catch again what sound had snatched him from his ponderings. But in this thickening haze the wild tangle of surrounding crags and hillslopes seemed wrapped in the brooding hush of centuries. From the south a coyote's yammer rose and fell, a dropped and ululating sound, like a fragment of something long gone and forgotten, rolling farther, dimmer, drearily off into the vast immensity of space.

For its duration Telldane sat there, a hard, cocked shape in his stockman's saddle. A wide gulch fell away before him, broadening in this deepening haze into the dun expanse of a yonder desert that stretched—these shadows made it seem—illimitably away into a dark and far horizon.

With a shrug he was about to wheel the roan around with some vague thought of angling back, searching out some recognized landmark, when a random wind whirled up and struck him—rooting him moveless with its smell of dust. On its heels the sound came, faint and far, but unmistakable. The rumbling bawl of driven cattle.

It was more like a memory than actual sound, and Bufe, scabbarding his rifle, slipped from the saddle and, taking the scarf from about his throat, unloosed its knot and spread it flat against the ground. Then, lying full length, he put his ear to it and when he rose a remote smile faintly edged his cheeks and fatigue's dull weight was forgotten feeling.

Quickly, grimly, he swung to the saddle. Cogged rowels bit and the blue roan jumped.

Ten minutes' run put the gulch behind them, saw them traveling the desert floor. It was not, Bufe saw now, a desert, really, but a long wide-arching flat hock-deep in dust, drab-studded with burro brush and cholla, with now and again some greasewood clump lifting yellow flowers to the fading light. Across its reach Bufe's eyes were fixed on a low, dark blur that years of stock detecting told him was a driven mass of strung out cattle.

He cut the flat at a racking tangent, drew up with an oath at the lip of a wash. Through the deepening haze his frowning glance picked out the gully's turn and wanderings; then, glance clearing, showing more hopeful, he urged the blue roan down its bank, went loping east along the bed's dry sand.

Turning, twisting, the wash led ever more steadily north. It was the way Bufe wanted to go and he was thankful he had had the wit to use it. The herd he'd seen was moving westward and sooner or later this wash would cross its path—unless it quit. And that was all right, too, he thought.

It was getting shallower fast now, and occasional views above its eroded banks showed the dark blotch of the herd much nearer; showed the drab expanse of the dusty flat to be merging into the richer soil of grazing lands. And suddenly Bufe saw against the tangle of nearing hills an upthrust spire he recognized. Apache Peak! The Fisk Mill road lay beyond it; and, somewhat farther, off to the left, Skull Mesa reared its table top. And atop Skull Mesa was Gann's headquarters . . . *that herd was headed for the dead man's ranch!*

Telldane knew in that moment the fate of Kerwold's vanishing cattle. The rustlers were using Gann's spread in their relay; first stop on the out-trail of Old Sam's cattle. They were held there probably till the brands healed over; rested and fattened, then drifted on, north and west, to New River. Sold there in small lots, the rustlers would have a ready, cash market. It was homesteader country; there'd be no questions asked.

140

Still traveling fast, Bufe scanned his chances. Too late now for help from Sam Kerwold; the Flying K lay south and east. Far—too far. They might not hold this bunch at Gann's—might drive straight through. He couldn't risk it. A good-sized herd, that one up ahead; all steers, very likely—cattle Sam couldn't afford to lose. He had to keep on. If he could stampede—

A sharp and upward slant of the ground took him out of the wash. A stand of timber lay dead ahead, perhaps three-quarters of a mile away; elsewhere all was rolling, manzanita-cluttered rangeland. The lancelike pole of a centinel yucca rose straight as a flagstaff off to the right and beyond it, not over a hundred yards, came the first wall-eyed steers of the bawling herd. The ground shook to their hooves and the rattle of horns made incessant clatter. Above these sounds came a rider's voice:

"Git on, y'u cow critters—hup thar! Hup—hup!"

With the rider's shout still traveling the dust, Bufe jerked the slicker from behind his cantle. One flick of the wrist set its folds gyrating. Whirling it round and round his head and yelling like a Comanche, he yanked out his six-shooter and with flame bright-spurting from its sky-aimed barrel he drove the roan straight at the herd.

He was seen!

A shouted oath sailed through the dust. The lead steers snorted, swerved and split. A long halloo shrilled through the shadows; other guns took up Bufe's challenge and muzzle lights streaked the swirling murk. But the herd was split, spilling off in two directions—which was something, but not enough. Be too easy for this crew to round them up again come daylight.

Using his spurs and keeping the roan straight at them, Bufe shoved the sixgun back in his belt, and a quick jerk dragged the Winchester across his saddlebow. Kicking his feet from the stirrups—still yelling—he dropped the tarp and, riding sharpshooter fashion, let drive three shots at the tangle of riders trying to force the cattle back in the trail.

One quick scream slid up a sobbing scale and choked. The frantic men before him melted, diving pellmell into the dust-streaked murk.

The cattle were definitely divided now—were scattering fast, breaking away in all directions; and he was almost onto them when the hatted head of a rider, then his shoulders—on Bufe's right—dimly cut the haze and sharpened. A lifted rifle jumped to his shoulder and the instant flame of it made a livid shaft reaching toward Bufe's saddle.

A stab of the rowels thrust the roan from its track. The close and flogging gait of horse hoofs jerked Telldane's attention from the man to see five riders pounding in, low bent across their saddles, their spitting guns dull-thudding against the din.

A whistling something tugged his neckerchief. Shock jarred through him as one bullet solidly struck the saddle horn. Then his lifted Winchester was barking answer and the nearest rider abruptly screeched and tumbled slanchways off his horse's pastern. And one more sagged, wildly clutching at the horn, before the rest of them took fright and, cursing, spurred for the timber.

Then a close call laid its track against his teeth, its sound bursting from the right of him, recalling vividly that other and forgotten rider.

Without thought Bufe flung his body low against the roan's left side, and beneath its neck saw the man coming in full tilt and, dropping his empty rifle, fired the last shot from his pistol—and knew he missed.

Flame fanned from the rider's gun in trip-hammered bursts of sound that washed cold chills across Bufe's neck; and then the roan's stride faltered—broke, and desperately Bufe dragged his boots from the stirrups and threw himself clear as the animal, heels over head, went down in a crashing fall.

Bufe lit on his shoulder and the whole world spun as momentum rolled him over and over.

He stopped against a catclaw's thorns, jerked clear and whirled, the useless pistol still clutched in his hand, to see the rider reining his bronc around forty feet away—come loping back to make sure his job was a good one.

All fingers, bathed in cold sweat, Bufe thumbed fresh loads from his belt. But knew before he got them loose he'd never fill the gun in time—and he didn't.

The rider, seeming to sense what Bufe was up to, loosed a mocking laugh and, stopping his bronc, drove three quick shots at point blank range and watchfully sat his saddle long moments after Bufe had fallen, before at last, with a jeering laugh, he reined away, riding after his pardners into the timber.

That laugh rang long in Telldane's ears. Only that instinctive ruse had saved him—that thought to fall when the man's gun lifted. Not one of those shots had touched him; but they'd come close—almighty close, and his scalp still crawled to the feel of their passing.

It was a good five minutes after the man had left before Bufe, shakily, rose to his feet and went to see if the roan were dead. It was. And a probing glance showed no other animals in sight—showed nothing save an empty range, for the cattle long since had gone, stampeded, and the departing rustlers seemed to have taken with them the two men he had dropped. He was afoot with a long night walk ahead of him; and as he refilled his empty pistol, this night's need decided him that he'd pack two in future.

But it was not of pistols that he thought as he prowled looking for his rifle. There was no room in his mind for guns. He had done Ab Holcomb an injustice in suspecting the man to be back of Kerwold's cattle losses. He wasn't—or he had not, leastways, been behind this attempt tonight.

That jeering laugh was still in Bufe's ears, still savaging his cheeks. In the gunflash of those final shots he had seen the face of the man who fired them. Andy Cooper, the fellow called himself; but Telldane knew him by the name of Blevins—a renegade who'd departed Texas a half jump ahead of the sheriff.

Well, things were due to happen, looked like.

They were—but not even in his wildest dreams could Bufe have foreseen the queer, fantastic turn those things were building up to take.

CHAPTER 19

FLAME OF DESIRE

DOG WEARY and dead on his feet, Telldane at eleven-fifteen lurched stiffly down the final slope and came into the yard at Ransome's Crossing like a man dragged through a knothole. A four-hour trek lay back of him—four miserable hours in high-heeled boots to a man long used to a saddle. These things were not conducive to thought, and letdown from that fight on the flat had ridden him hard—unstrung him. All his nerves were jangling as he swayed there, one hand braced against the cottonwood's bole, stupidly eying the yellow bars of light coming out of the storefront windows.

Drained of emotion—physically and mentally exhausted as he was, habit still retained its hold on him. For three years he been geared to the need for caution and that need stayed with him now. He was doggedly bending his steps toward the door when that need stopped him, reawakened by sight of the horse that was hitched to the porch rail. A strange horse—a long-legged, jug-headed bay.

Bufe stood there shaking his head, trying to clear his mind of its cobwebs and, in some measure, he was successful.

Voice sound was coming from the store, low-held, an unintelligible mutter that yet held some odd cadence that tugged at Bufe's dulled memory. Man's talk it was; and he wondered who could be calling on the Ransomes at that hour. The thought came to him that he might go inside and see; and he was starting when the man's voice sharpened and hard on its heels there came a thud as of something falling and a quick, scared cry from Holly.

It was the last that roused him.

Stopping, he canted his head and listened. The man was speaking again, a wicked satisfaction in his tones—a kind of gloating. The sound of it grated across Bufe's nerves like a file, stiffening his shoulders and bringing him to a full awareness. The speaker was Topock—Cooper's pardner.

Weariness forgotten, Telldane's storeward progress was a smooth and soundless thing. The lines of his cheeks were couched in bleakness, and a cold, malicious purpose before he reached the steps moved him to briefly pause and shove fresh loads in his pistol. It was while he was engaged in this that Holly screamed; and, instantly, through that scream the labored sound of struggling bodies came to clear his mind like magic.

147

Three strides took him raggedly across the porch and a blow from his boot flung back the door, banging it violently against the inside wall.

For all his avowed intention, Gus Pring did not ride home with Kerwold. They had gone a bare two miles from Holcomb's spread when the Double Bar Circle boss pulled up with a cool apology. "Sorry, Sam, but I've got to go back. Some business I forgot to finish with Ab—a horse deal I better close before the fool changes his mind. Look—I'll see you later. Give Jane my regrets and tell her I'll drop by this evening."

Holcomb did not receive Pring's return with any great display of enthusiasm. "You played hell, you did, rubbin' salt into Telldane that way—far's that goes, you've fixed things all around. I'd just got through tellin' him I wa'n't expectin' nobody when you threw that bull shout down the hall—"

"To hell with that," Pring cut him off. "He ain't goin' to be botherin' us long—"

"I've heard that remark before. Been spoke by smarter guys'n you, too—but where are them guys now? By grab, I wisht I was out of this!"

"What's the matter—yellow?"

Holcomb gave him a long regard. "I guess you know better'n that, Gus. We been through enough tights together. But God knows—"

"You always was an old woman, Ab. Trouble with you is, you get the shakin' palsy every time that guy's name is mentioned. Fixed him up in Texas, didn't we?"

Holcomb shrugged, squatted down by the steps, made aimless curlycues in the dirt with a blunt and calloused index finger. He growled without looking up, "Was that what you borried that money for?"

"What are you off on now—"

"You know what I mean. Is it like Sam said—that you borried from the bank to beat him outa Wildcat?"

Pring considered a moment. "An' what if it is?"

Holcomb made more marks. "I wouldn't of backed you in that, Gus. Sam's been a good friend to me—been a pretty good friend to you, too, if what I've heard is right. The bargain was, we was to leave Flyin' K alone—"

The lines of Pring's big shoulders stiffened. A change rode across his cheeks and he said bluntly: "Get this straight. I've got nothing personal against Sam Kerwold or any other guy round here; but long's I got a shot in the locker the plans we made are goin' ahead. The Boxed Double A Cattle Syndicate is goin' to control this country—from Long Valley clean on south to Hell's Hip Pocket; and any spread that won't play along with us is headin' for the skids! I've sounded Sam, an' talkin' to him about syndicates is like red-flaggin' a bull. Sam's a doddern' old has-been—last bulwark of a gone-by era. Long as his Jack-in-the-Beanstalk notions don't interfere with our business, he can go to Halifax for all of me. But the minute they do—"

Holcomb said protestingly: "But tryin' for Wildcat—"

"Tryin' for Wildcat is interference. Long as I saw the chance, it was my intention to take Wildcat away from him—"

"I thought you was sweet on Sam's daughter—"

"We'll leave Jane out of this," Pring snapped; and changed the subject. "Last time we talked together I laid down certain lines for you to work on. One of 'em concerned that precious brother of yours—have you found out where he stands?"

Ab Holcomb sighed. "I'm afraid he's swingin' with Topock." He stared morosely at the marks he had made in the dust. He said abruptly: "What you figurin' to do now Topock's fixed it so them Wildcat lands—"

"Lease from the homesteaders."

"Maybe Topock won't—"

"Then Topock will have to go—like Sam or anyone else that gets in my way."

Holcomb shook his head. "You're bitin' off—"

"What I bite off I can chew," Pring said and stepped up on the porch. "There's something on your desk I—"

"Figure you can chew Telldane?"

150

"Bah!" Pring's shoulders stirred impatiently. "You got Telldane on the brain!"

"Guess I have. 'Nough to get on anyone's brain—anyone that's got one."

There was something sinister, something wolf-ish, in the grin that tugged Pring's lips. "You can give the brain a rest," he said; "Bufe won't be botherin' us long."

Holcomb thought about it all the time Gus was in the house; and when the man stepped out on the porch again he was buttoning the gabardine flap of his pocket. But Holcomb, still busy with his thoughts, didn't notice. That the thoughts held little of pleasure was evidenced by the dis-satisfied set of his cheeks. He said uneasily: "Just the same, Gus, I'd feel better if you'd leave Sam out of—"

"We're not going over that again."

Holcomb sighed. "I wisht," he said, "I'd known all this—"

"You went into it with your eyes open—you knew what the syndicate was formed for. You were as keen—"

"I didn't know about Telldane then, an' I didn't suppose—"

"Too bad. Any time you don't see eye to eye with my plans and policies, you can pick up your blocks and go home."

Quietly spoken though they were, there was a crisp finality in Pring's words that stopped

151

Ab Holcomb's protests. He'd encountered that finality before. In fact, there'd been many times since their secret partnership had been established that Holcomb had wished himself out of it. But he could not get out—Pring had him, lock, stock and barrel. There was a clause in their agreement—like the death clause that was in it—that if for any reason either party tried to break himself out of the contract, all that party's property—livestock, land and buildings, went unequivocally to the surviving partner, and there'd been several occasions here of late that had made Ab wonder if he'd collect any profit at all.

With the dress half ripped from her shoulders, backed against the wall, with arms hard braced against the Texan's chest, across Topock's shoulder as the door slammed back Holly saw the white clamped cheeks of Bufe Telldane.

The room gyrated wildly as Topock in a sweating haste roughly whirled her away from him as he spun to face the door. She reeled and stumbled, hearing him curse horribly. And when from hands and knees she looked up from the floor she found him crouched by the overturned cracker box, face blanched, eyes bright with terror as they stared, uncontrollably fascinated, at the gun in Telldane's hand.

He was afraid of Bufe! His fear was unmistakable, laying sheer and stark in his widesprung eyes, in the cringing of his muscles, slack lips and stiffened figure.

She watched them breathless, looking first at one and then the other.

A malicious smile curved Telldane's lips, abruptly pulling them back from his teeth. There was hatred in that smile and a rage that was deep and bitter. He seemed plainly aware of Topock's terror; it deepened the contempt in his eyes and shaped the grimness of his cheeks to lines of cold derision.

He did not speak, just stood and looked, seeming to await some word from the burly Texan. Where was all Topock's courage now? All that reckless, swaggering bravado he displayed so readily to women? Where was all the confidence his former bold talk had indicated?

Perhaps Topock thought of this himself, for his shoulders straightened and he made some pretense of courage. He said, scowling: "What do *you* want—an' what's the idea of that gun? Tryin' to scare somebody?"

However he may have intended the words to sound, they succeeded only in being bombastic; and they did not fool the man in the door, and Topock could see they didn't. The knowledge did little to bolster the impression he sought to give; indeed, it seemed to Holly Ransome that his cheeks went even paler, if that were possible, than they had been before.

He cleared his throat, licked nervously at dry lips. "If this is a bluff—"

"It's no bluff, Topock. You've reached the end of your rope. If you got anything to say, you better say it quick."

It looked like Topock had a lot he wanted to say, but the words seemed to stick in his throat. His dry lips moved, but no sound came—no sound that was intelligible.

Telldane's smile was coldly derisive. "Time's up," he said. "You've got a gun on you—use it."

Silence, brittle and complete, shut down on the heels of his words. It was a horribly tense and terrifying interval during which the girl was gripped by the icy chill of paralysis. So, apparently, was Topock. He made a stiff and awkward shape, half crouched as he was; his mouth hung open, gaping, and the eyes seemed starting from his head.

"You—you—*I can't!*"

"What's the matter with you—crippled? You looked all right when I came in." Telldane said with curling lips: "Quite natural, in fact."

Holly found her voice. She said: "It—it's all right, Dane. He hasn't hurt me—"

"I'm glad to hear it."

He might have been—but you could not have proved it by that tone. Nor by the look of him, either. He did not take his eyes from Topock. He said with a bleakness not to be missed: "How long you been in this country, hombre?"

The Texan made three tries before he finally got his voice to working. Even then it was just a mumble. "Three weeks—"

"Hmm. Been pretty busy, haven't you? Little *too* busy, I'd say, because it seems like you been overlooking something—something that's got considerable bearin' on the—er—state of your—ah—health."

"What's all that yap supposed to mean?" growled Topock, showing again some measure of his old belligerence. He seemed to have read into Telldane's delay some basis for relief; and with the relief came confidence. He said, sneering, "What'd I overlook?"

A corner of Telldane's mouth twitched as though a cold smile lurked just back of it. "Haven't you ever heard there's a code in this country, Topock?"

The Texan stiffened. Dull color edged into his cheeks, bloating the jowls of him poisonously. "What are you talkin' about?" he snarled.

"The code of the Tonto, Topock—the unwritten laws of this country. There's one of 'em's got considerable bearin' on your conduct—on what's goin' to happen to you, likewise."

Topock went stock still. The eyes in his stark white face were like burnt holes in a yellow blanket.

Holly, too, appeared to grasp the implication. Dread of what those words implied rushed her into headlong speech. "But he never touched me!" she protested. "I've *told* you! He hasn't done anything—"

Telldane paid no attention. He was watching Topock with a cold, banked interest; and the bleakness of that stare abruptly set the Texan shaking. He trembled like a gale-struck aspen and a great sweat clammed his forehead—stood in bright beads across his lips. A long, rattling breath rushed out of him and he quavered in abject terror: "Great Christ! I didn't mean nothin'—*Honest to God I didn't!*"

And Holly stormed at Bufe desperately: "I forbid you to do this thing—I forbid you! Bufford Dane, do you *hear* me? I've not been hurt and you shan't use me as an excuse to do murder! Don't you *dare* to shoot him!"

Telldane turned then, swept her with a grim regard. The gleam of his eyes brought a crimson flush to her throat. As she went back a pace, his smile held a mocking malice. "I don't need any excuse for murder—I thought you knew that, ma'am. I—"

The look of her eyes must have warned him.

Mouth closing, he whirled to find Guy Topock with a lifted gun in his fist. White flame leaped out of its muzzle and from Telldane's hip an answering light burst raggedly. Two shots roared as one, shaking the walls with their tumultuous clamor; and the lamplight, wildly flaring, showed the Texan with his wabbly knees buckling under him, pitching forward across the oiled floor.

They were like that, with the smoke still wreathing lazily from the barrel of Telldane's pistol, when from the open door behind them a cold voice said malevolently: "Don't move, Telldane—don't move at all. We've got you dead to rights this time!"

CHAPTER 20

Lou Safford Plays His Hand

THE yard at Brill's was filled with riders—grim-eyed, muttering, angry men. Cooper's rustlers, just returned from the raid on Kerwold, the raid whose profits had been stampeded by Bufe Telldane. Cooper swung out of his saddle savagely. "Come inside, you!" he snarled at Tim Ransome, and clanked across Brill's creaking porch. At the door he paused, called over his shoulder: "Rest of you birds stay where you are. Keep your eyes peeled an' stay in the saddle; we'll be ridin' again in just a few minutes."

Tim Ransome followed him into the place, stood restless, uneasy, while Cooper lit the lamp. Then Cooper turned and his cheeks were wicked. "Don't know why in the hell I keep you on. You're no more use'n a busted gut! You know who it was stampeded them cattle?"

"I—I guess it was Telldane, wasn't it?"

"You know it was Telldane, damn you! Didn't Topock tell you to get him? Didn't he tell you he'd cancel them I.O.U.'s if you'd down

158

Telldane? Well, why ain't you done it? Eh? Answer, you whelp!"

Ransome, shifting weight, nervously licked dry lips. "I—I—"

"Ahr," Cooper snarled. "If I'd no more sand in my craw than you've got, I'd sure as hell cut my throat!"

Ransome bridled. He said defensively: "I ain't no match for a—"

"Don't talk foolishness," Cooper snapped. "Nobody asked you to go up against him—a shot from the rimrock would've done the trick—"

"I tried that!" Ransome blurted. "Twice I tried—"

"Then you're a damn poor shot!" Cooper scowled malevolently. "I'm goin' to give you one last chance—"

"To hell with you!" Ransome threw back at him. "You can shove them I.O.U.'s up your pants-leg for all of me—I'm through with this outfit! *Through*—do you hear?"

Cooper stared. His laugh was ugly. "Well, well, well! So you're through, are you? Listen to me, you spineless jackrabbit—there ain't nobody bunch-quittin' on me! *Nobody!*"

Ransome glared back at him sulkily. "I won't try for Tell—"

"You won't need to. Telldane's dead—I killed him tonight. Kerwold's the bird you're goin' to line your sights on. An' you better not do no more missin', neither!" He grinned at the look on Ransome's blanched features.

"Kerwold!"

"You bet! It's high time—"

"Are you crazy?"

"Like a fox," Cooper sneered. "He's been messin' things up long enough—*too* long. You drop him tomorrow, or tomorrow night I'm puttin' a flea in Lou Safford's ear."

Ransome wiped his face on his sleeve; with a visible effort got hold of himself. "Lou Safford quit the Basin a week ago—"

"You got a lot to learn," Cooper sneered. "Safford's been trackin' that first batch of homesteaders. He got back this morning . . ." Some thought scowled up his rawboned cheeks and he snapped gruffly: "You get Duarte Vargas, too, while you're out there. That bastard's playin' some game of his own—the doublecrossin' sneak rubbed out those tracks himself, an' by God he'll be paid for his antics. I don't know what his game is an' I don't give a damn; you get him an' get Sam Kerwold, an' don't come back till you do!"

Ransome began protestingly, "I—"

Cooper's fist lashed out, struck Ransome with a meaty impact that drove him reeling against the bar. With blood dripping off his chin he cowered there, shaking, whimpering.

"Get up on your feet, you drivelin' scissorsbill! What Topock ever roped you into this for—

More of his goddam smartness, I guess! You do what I tell you! Either you rub them two out or tomorrow night I tell Lou Safford you're boss of the night riders workin' these hills! Get out of here now—get over there an' get holed up where you can drop 'em first thing in the morning."

Recognition of that voice cocked Telldane's muscles and left him stiff-placed, moveless. Behind him somewhere stood Lou Safford. Lou Safford of the long-fingered hands and racking cough—Safford, the Basin marshal.

If Telldane realized the futility of action, if he concluded from the other's words that he was trapped, his face, it must be admitted, did not publicize the fact. His expression was wholly grave; but it was calm, too, unperturbed—almost tranquil, one might have said. No evidence of fear was in it. No worry edged his cheeks.

He said, ignoring the ominous timbre of the other's voice, "Oh—Hello, Lou," and sliding the big pistol into its sheath, stepped over against the counter and, turning, put the flats of his hands upon it and regarded the lawman with a composure that was baffling.

Safford glared. Blood suffused his neck above the string tie at his throat and, mounting, spread across his face in a swiftly darkening tide that did not half do justice to his outraged sense of propriety. His black eyes snapped with anger and

161

he snarled, half choked, choleric: "Unbuckle that belt and drop it! Telldane, you're under arrest!"

"For what?"

The marshal swore and the two men with him smiled thinly. "You got the gall to ask me that?" Lou Safford's cheeks were mottled.

Telldane said mildly, "If you mean for this"—and he waved a hand round the room—"you're goin' off half-cocked, I'm afraid. I didn't kill the old man there—I expect Guy Topock struck him with a gun, or maybe his fist. If you don't care to believe me, ask Miz Holly; an' anyhow he isn't dead. As for Topock—"

"Yes?" It was a sneer the way Lou said it.

Telldane grinned at him bleakly. "I sure killed *him* all right."

"Got an alibi all pat for that, too, have you?"

"You don't need an alibi for killin' a skunk."

Change ripped across Lou Safford's face. "Get peeled of that gun belt an' hurry it up."

Bufe Telldane, without moving, drawled: "I'll have to know why I'm arrested first."

The marshal scowled at him wickedly but Telldane, coolly indifferent, shrugged. "It'll save time, Lou, if you tell me."

One of the men with Safford growled. The other man spat and, shifting his cud, said belligerently: "Want we should bust 'im for you, Lou?"

It pulled Bufe's lips apart in a grin. He folded brown arms across his chest and leaned against the counter comfortably. Holly was on her knees nearby, working over her father anxiously. But Telldane did not look at her; his regard stayed on the marshal coolly, and the blacker grew Lou Safford's cheeks, the more amused Bufe's smile became.

The affair was at a deadlock. There was a pistol ready in Safford's fist but a certain gleam in Bufe's level eyes seemed to warn how far he could go with it. The men with the marshal stirred impatiently, but still Lou Safford stood and looked; angry, resentful, dark-scowling but cautious.

Bufe Telldane unfolded his arms. Hooking thumbs in gun belt, he said; "Come, Lou—let's get this over an' done with. You figure to grab me for downin' Topock?"

But Safford, at last, seemed to have made up his mind. "To hell with Topock," he ground out brashly. "You murdered Jess Brill an' by God you'll swing for it!"

Marvelingly, Bufe Telldane swore. "So it's Brill you're after me for . . . Jess Brill! You're claimin' I murdered *Brill?*"

The marshal sneered and his men sneered with him. "Never mind the act! I know what I know—an' you know it, too! You was goddam careless *that* time, bucko; your gloves was found on the ground beside him!"

Telldane stared. "My gloves . . ."

163

"Unbuckle that belt—*I'm no damn' fool!* Holcomb will swear to 'em. So will Pring. I guess you ain't callin' Gus Pring no liar!"

"He's the soul of honor," Bufe said sarcastically; and suddenly Safford went stiff and still and the two men with him stood rigid as statues at something they read in Bufe Telldane's stare.

He shoved free of the counter, stood tall and grim. " 'Fraid I can't surrender tonight, Lou," he said. "Seems there's a couple loose chores I've forgot—"

"You bust out of here," the marshal snarled, "an' I'll get you outlawed for the rest of your life!"

Telldane's smile was a thing of the lips. "Be like old times—me ridin' the river. But," he said, soft-drawled, "I guess that's the way it'll have to be, Lou. Step over there—"

"Get him, boys!" Lou Safford cried and went for his gun, the other two with him.

White flame leaped twice from Telldane's hip. An oath, a screech, and the lamp snuffed out. Its last wild flare showed the marshal reeling. Then a thundering dark had the place in its grip—a blackness crisscrossed by the burst of burnt powder, alive with the whispering scream of thrown lead.

The place still throbbed with its crashing echoes when hoof sound flogged a rushed tattoo that beat swiftly upward, died away in the hills.

CHAPTER 21

"THEN I'D CALL YOU TO YOUR FACE—"

FOR three solid weeks posses under Deputy Sheriff 'Deef' Smith scoured the basin country in search of Bufe Telldane. At times there were over half a hundred men out, prowling the crags and canyons, for Marshal Lou Safford was 'gone to his just rewards' and the county had offered a $2,000 bounty for the apprehension of his killer—who was also charged with the murders of Brill and Topock. Bufe Telldane was making history again; and Gila County aimed to do likewise if it could ever get its hands on him.

The deputy, Deef Smith—so called because of his unfailing habit of making you ask him everything twice before he would undertake to answer, was a tall man, built like a hitching post and sporting floppy ears that stuck out from the sides of his head just like the ears of a donkey. In fact, everything about him seemed either to flop or to flap—the holster that was slung at his hip, the points of his pinto vest, the flaring flaps of his batwing chaps and the whang strings he had tied to him everywhere. His age was somewhere between fifty and sixty and he had the reputation of being a considerable sight more stubborn than a mule; and in the pursuit of Bufe Telldane he appeared doing his damndest to prove it.

He had no business around Wildcat Hill, for it was fifteen miles into Maricopa, but he frequently showed there anyway and the slant of his lantern jaw promised trouble if anyone looked like making something of it. Bob Lally, Maricopa's sheriff, just winked at folks that brought him this news. "Well, well!" he said, and that ended it.

So, all across that broken country, Smith drove his farflung posses. Not once did they sight the fugitive or even so much as cut sign of him. Telldane had vanished. There was no getting round it; and finally, reluctantly, Smith disbanded his men. But he did not give up the hunt.

"He'll be back," he told enquirers; "an' when he comes back I'll git him!"

But if things stood still in the sheriffing business, no such impasse blocked the basin war. Raid and counter-raid followed each other in rapid succession. Kerwold was fighting back now, and every time one of his camps were raided, or more fence was destroyed, or more cattle stolen, dire consequences were attendant upon the property of some small cowman. Up-river, at Oak Spring Canyon, a squatter caught riding solo by a group of unidentified masked horsemen was promptly hoisted to a cottonwood limb and left dangling as a warning to others. Southeast, below Bee Mountain, two masked riders shot a homesteader down on his doorstep and curtly told the widow to "load up your stuff an' git out of here!" Gann's ranch was fired, all its buildings burned to the ground; the corrals and pens and chutes were destroyed, and the bulk of Gann's stock was run off. No man could say who had done it, but with Gann dead and no heir apparent, his riders—what were left of them—took the hint and departed. Young Tim Ransome, too, appeared to have quit the country; he had not been seen since the night of Guy Topock's killing. Considerable speculation was rife as to the cause of Topock's killing; and even Lou Safford's death was surrounded by an aura of mystery. True, his deputies swore that Telldane had yanked a gun and shot him while in process of being apprehended for the cold-blooded murder of Brill. But the wise ones of the country shook their heads; and there were knowing glints in more than one pair of eyes. How come, the question was asked, that both Topock and Safford had been killed in the Ransome store? What had they been doing there that night? "You notice," folks pointed out, "them deputies ain't shootin' off their jaws none about why Telldane gunned Topock!" And this appeared cause for more headshaking—as did the lack of all comment on the part of the Ransomes, father and daughter.

There sure was a nigger in the woodpile some-place!

But if there were, it stayed there. And after a time, for lack of fuel, most of the talk died out.

And then one night a solitary horseman rode down from the hills and knocked on the Kerwold door.

Jane Kerwold herself came to open it; and stepped back with a low, choked cry.

Bufe Telldane's bow was a brief, curt thing. The eyes in his gaunted face were bleak and the dust of long trails grimed his clothing. He said gruffly: "If Sam's around, I'd like to see him a minute."

She stood there, shrinking back from him, one hand at her throat, eyes dark and round and staring. Some unknown thinking then worried her cheeks and she said breathlessly, almost anxiously: "Quick! Step in here out of the light!" and held the screen door open.

He stepped past her with curling lips, for he knew her anxiety was caused by fear that someone seeing him would lay the blame for his presence on Kerwold. He said with a sneer in his voice: "I won't be here but a minute. I don't reckon anyone's followed me."

She looked at him queerly, he thought—seemed about to say something. But she must have changed her mind for, with a little nod, she hurried off; and pretty soon Old Sam's heavy step preceded him into the hall.

"By God, boy, I thought they'd run you out of the country," Sam said, and winked as he held out his hand.

"Listen," Bufe said, "put this in your safe—it's your lease for the Wildcat—"

Sam took it, dubiously eying him. "I'm obliged as hell," he said gruffly. "I realize it's entirely my fault you're—"

"You didn't have anything to do with it. I shot Guy Topock because he needed shooting, and I gunned Safford because he was trying to frame me—and there's one more guy I'm squaring up with before I take to the timber. You needn't feel responsible for my troubles at all. Now look—get your steers onto Wildcat right away an'—"

"Just a second," Sam said, and rasped a hand across his jowls reluctantly. "I hate to say it, an' I don't want you to figure I'm not appreciatin' what you've tried to do for me, but—the truth is, Bufe, I don't see how this lease of yours can do me a mite of good, now. You've filed on it under the Homestead Act an' you've got to do your work on it in order to get your rights; an' how're you goin' to do that with half the country doggin' your sign? Hell, boy, they'll prob'ly cross your name off the books, now you been made a outlaw." He stared at Telldane earnestly. "I hate

169

like sin to say it, but I guess we've plumb lost Wildcat."

"You're still wanting that lease, ain't you?"

"Wantin' it? Hell, I got to *have* it if I—"

"O.K., then, get your cattle onto it. Until they scratch me off the books this paper covers you— an' beyond, I shouldn't wonder. With this paper in your hands you can tie Wildcat up in the courts for years if you got to."

"Yeah . . . But you're forgettin' mebbe that there's a whole lot of other fellers needin' that land. Christ, boy, I'd need an army to keep my cows in that grass!"

Bufe grinned across at him bleakly. "You get your critters onto it an' leave the rest up to me."

Kerwold stared, stepped back aghast. "My God! You ain't figurin' to stay on in this country are you?"

"I'll stick as long as I can," Bufe said, and changed the subject. "Ever hear of an outfit called the Boxed Double A?"

Old Sam looked thoughtful; shook his head. "Located in this—"

Telldane nodded, darkly scowling. "The brand's listed in this county. I got an idee they been usin' Gann's place in their business. Look here—"

He crossed to Kerwold's desk, picked up a piece of paper and, with a stub of pencil dug from his pocket, swiftly made a couple sketches. Sam's Flying K brand and, alongside of it, the imprint of the Boxed Double A. He paused then, tipped his head, and looked at Sam Kerwold grimly.

Kerwold looked from Bufe to the brands and suddenly his eyes showed a bitter glint and his cheeks darkened up with anger. Telldane nodded. "Wouldn't take any great shucks with an iron to cover your brand with this one."

Kerwold said thickly: "Where's this outfit located?"

"They got a P. O. box at the county seat." Bufe's grin was hard and meaningful.

"Whose name's it in?"

"Same one that's listed in the brand book—Boxed Double A Cattle Syndicate."

"It's a Goddam rustlers' brand!"

"Sure it is. Been started to take care of your surplus. S'pose it could be this fellow Cooper? Cooper an' Topock, mebbe?"

"But Topock's dead—"

"He wasn't when this brand was recorded."

They stared at each other thoughtfully. Bufe said: "I've been scoutin' round since I been on the dodge an' I've found out two or three things. It was Topock got your $2,000 off the stage that night. Turned most of it over to Cooper to pay off Cooper's night riders—"

"Raiders?" Sam said sharply.

Telldane nodded "Cooper an' Topock may not have started this Boxed Double A—or, again, they may have. But one thing I can tell

171

you certain: Cooper's bossin' a band of range roughers that are levyin' hard on your cattle—I caught 'em at it the night I killed Topock. They was headed for Gann's place when I stampeded 'em."

Kerwold stood a long while in thought. He said, looking up abruptly: "You the one that fired Gann's spread?"

Telldane grunted a negative. "I been wonderin' about that fire myself. Did you know Gann an' Holcomb was brothers?"

"Hell, no!"

"Well, they were," Bufe said, and told him of the conversation he'd had with Ab Holcomb. "I forgot an' left my gloves at his place that morning— don't suppose you recollect seein' 'em there, do you? I left them on Ab's desk, I think . . .."

But Kerwold shook his head. His mind seemed too filled with other things to be worried about Telldane's gloves. He said irritably: "I swear I'm so tangled in my mind I don't know up from down. But heavens an' earth! If Gann an' Holcomb was brothers, an' you caught Cooper's crowd drivin' some of my Flyin' K's towards Gann's Skull Mesa ranch, I'd say by God that the whole lousy bunch of 'em was ganged up to put me out of business!"

"It might be," Telldane admitted, "that they've all been workin' towards that end—it's a cinch Topock an' Cooper was the ones that got them

172

homesteaders in here, an' that Gann was mixed up with them in that part of it, but . . . Well, frankly, Sam, I don't think Holcomb's connected with 'em."

He scowled at the desktop growningly. "That fellow Vargas round anyplace, Sam?"

Kerwold's look got intent, suspicious. "I told you once—"

Telldane waved it aside. "If he's round, suppose you call him in here—"

"Never mind—"

"As a favor, Sam," Telldane said gravely.

Kerwold eyed him stiffly, grimly. With a long hard roll of the shoulders, he strode to the door, stepped out on the porch. Bufe heard his bull voice sail across the yard—heard somebody muttering an answer.

Sam came in and shut the door. Stood with his back against it, frowning.

"Not around, eh?" Telldane drawled. "I didn't think he would be. Find out where he's gone?"

There was a hard-held look to Kerwold's cheeks and his tone was flat, unconfiding. "Cook said he rode off someplace after supper."

"Let's have the cook in here for a minute."

Sam yanked open the door and called him; and a few moments later the cook stepped in. His eyes sprang wide when he saw Telldane.

Bufe said: "That a habit of Vargas's—ridin' off after supper?"

173

The man's glance jumped to Kerwold. "Go ahead. Answer him," Sam said gruffly.

The cook still hesitated. He said nervously, "Well, uh . . . That is to say—"

"Is it or ain't it?"

"I ain't been payin' no special attention," the man said finally. "I got my own work to do an'—"

"Joe," Old Sam cut in harshly, "I got my back against the wall. Answer this fellow's question. If you've noticed anything—umm—*peculiar* about Vargas's actions, right now's a good time to mention it."

The cook's grizzled cheeks got a little pink. "I don't know's I have," he grumbled. "But some of the boys has been layin' bets lately about who Duarte's settin' the bag for. Seems they've noticed sev'ral mornin's late-like that that black geldin' of his has been showin' signs of night work—"

"I think that's all we want to know," Bufe said to Kerwold; and Sam nodded to the cook who, still looking uncomfortable, forthwith departed.

Bufe said nothing. Kerwold, after a hard, bitter stare at him, growled: "Looks like you might be right about him at that. Mebbe I had better look into his doings a little—"

"Better watch your step if you do, Sam. The fellow's no Bible-tract salesman. Better take things easy—give him plenty of rope an' keep your eyes peeled. Be a good idea to find out what his game is before you jump him . . . Well," he said with a shrug for the unconvinced look on Kerwold's face, "I guess I better be driftin'—"

"You're goin' to stick, then?"

"Long as I can."

"You watch out for Deef Smith, then—that guy's a hunter from who cocked the trigger—contrary as a mule an' stubborn as Job's boils. He'll hang to your tracks like glue, boy, an' if he ever sights you down a rifle—"

"I'll watch out for him."

He was climbing into the saddle when somebody stepped from the shadows, laid a detaining hand on his arm. Looking round, Bufe found Jane Kerwold facing him.

"Bufe—"

"Well?" Telldane said it coldly.

"Bufe, I—"

"All that's past," Bufe told her harshly, forestalling what she might have said. "Water under the bridge. You needn't worry—I'll keep my mouth shut."

The light was bad, but even so he could see how her shoulders stiffened. His words had hurt, and he had meant them to. She had tricked him once—played him for a sucker. He'd no intention of having the experience repeated. "If it's in your head I followed you here, you can get shut of that

175

idea pronto—I'd never have come within miles of this place if I'd known you were Old Sam's daughter!"

"I believe you," she said quietly after a moment. "You *do* hate me, don't you?"

Bufe didn't bother answering that one.

"I suppose it would be useless for me to try to explain—"

"Complete waste of breath!"

Through the shadows he saw her shoulders droop, felt her hand withdrawn from his arm. But she did not go, not at once. She said, voice so low he scarce could hear her, "But it's so senseless, Bufe! If you'd only listen—"

"I've listened too long already," he sneered. "Nothing you could tell me would change my notions a fraction—I know what I know and that's the end of it. Do you think, after—after what I saw that night, that—"

"Not even if I said that I still loved you? That—that I had *always* loved you and that what you—"

"What I inadvertently walked in on?" Bufe inquired sarcastically.

She half turned away and then her chin came up and she said determinedly: "Yes! That what you inadvertently walked in on had been deliberately pre—"

"Then I'd call you to your face what I've known you really are ever since that night—a lying, selfish, miserable little cheat! *Is that*

176

plain?" Bufe's laugh was short, an ugly sound. He said, "Now get out of my way. I've got to ride and I'm in a hurry."

He did not wait for her to move aside but, swinging into the saddle, he savagely wheeled the horse that had been Lou Safford's, and feeding it steel, quit the place at a hard fast run.

CHAPTER 22

GUN THUNDER

QUITTING the Flying K yard, Telldane rode blindly, giving the horse its way, his mind a seething maelstrom of wild thoughts and tortuous imaginings. Conflicting passions tore at him, and a cold sweat clammed his brow as, furiously, he recognized what an attraction the girl still had for him. This was the truth—the bitter and humiliating truth. Despite all he knew against her, despite all he'd suffered at her hands, Jane Kerwold still had the power to move him, to cause his pulses to leap and bound, to upset completely the traditionally cool and will-governed run of his mind. A thousand thoughts besieged him, all centering around the vital and compelling figure of this girl, the purl of her voice—its husky cadence, her ways—each manner and gesture, the cut of her profile, the slant of her cheeks and the remembered turquoise blue of her eyes—these, all these, were before him, crystal clear with yesterday's poignance. Three years he'd gone a headlong way trying to sear these things from memory only to find, tonight, that they were stronger, more compelling than ever before.

It was a curse laid on him for the turbulence he'd embraced to forget them. He was like the man in the poem, with the dead duck hung round his neck.

For he saw with a hateful clarity now that he was still in love; *in love*—God save the mark!—with a girl who had used him contemptibly—and seemed even now seeking so to use him again!

Where was his pride? he thought with blanching cheeks. God—had the world ever known such fool as Bufe Telldane! Telldane, the man who had always prided himself on the steeled control of his emotions! In love with a girl who had cared so little as to make of his passion a mockery—a subject for hoots and scoffing!

He jeered at and berated himself; jeered at her, at what might have been. He sneered and cursed—consigned her to hell; but it made him feel little better. The truth was there to ridicule him, to flog and scourge and ride him. His passion burned with a bright white light. No abuse, no reviling, could quench it.

What a poor, puny husk of a man he was! To care with such undiminished passion—to *care at all* for one who could hold that regard in so low esteem. He must be soft in the head! He must—

Through his concerned absorption, scattering his disjointed reflections like chaff before a gale, came the flogged hoof sound of a horse that was running like mad. The racing pound of those hoofs bit through the night like a tocsin.

Head up, eyes narrowed to the warning of that sound, Telldane reined his horse from the trail. Wheeled into a thicket of squatting cedar, he crouched, forward-leaning from the saddle, waiting, with all his screaming nerves yanked tight, a pistol gripped in his hand.

Downslope tumbled echoes of that crashing gait drove jouncing and bouncing—a roll of doom; unreasoning, monstrous, a cacophony of sound.

Out of the darkness lunged a horse with nostrils flaring, ears flattened, foam flecked, its wild eyes glaring. Half out of the saddle—but clinging still with the clutch of death—showed its rider, hatless, hair flying, his whiskers whipped by that whirlwind pace, vest flapping, wind-bellied shirt all stains and tatters.

A name leaped stiff from Telldane's lips. *"Ab Holcomb!"* he cried, and spurred his horse after them.

But a frenzy of terror drove Holcomb's horse; and spur and quirt though Bufe would and did, nothing it seemed but miles could close that thundering gap between them. And then Holcomb fell—Bufe saw him go; out of the saddle and off the trail, over and over like a sack of spilled meal. Ab's body brought up in a greasewood clump; and then Bufe was down on a knee, beside him.

The Straddle Bug boss was not dead nor out. A wan grin twisted the colorless lips; then a rasping, choking gasp—a cough, rattled the breath hung up in his throat, and he shivered in Bufe's supporting grip. His head fell forward, chin digging his chest. But mumbled sound squeezed through his teeth and Bufe, bent close, caught the muttered words.

When he rose, sweat beaded the slant of Bufe's cheeks; they were white, stiff-clamped. His mouth was a gash. Ab Holcomb lay dead in the brush at his feet—but not in vain. His words rang like trumpets in Bufe's reeling brain. The truth—the staggering, ghastly truth—was his at last.

Duarte Vargas, at Flying K, got off his horse by the pole corral and stood a moment in the pooled gloom, thinking. He knew the crew was out on the range, for he'd given the order himself, after supper. There'd be nobody round but the cook and Old Sam—and the girl, of course; but she didn't matter.

Duarte Vargas was a cold-blooded man; a thinking, scheming, far-sighted man who could see the main chance and had the wit to grab it. He was a close, tight-fisted man as well and had a goodly store of hard money laid by, the savings of fifteen years of ramrod's pay, augmented these last two years by the secret addition of checks from a neighbor.

He had a laugh for the expression that must have stamped that neighbor's face could he have known what he, Duarte Vargas, was intending now. That man wanted power, the control of this basin; and for two years Vargas had taken pay for helping him. But he was through with that now. They had reached, this neighbor and Vargas, the parting of the ways. Vargas was through with helping someone else; from here on out he meant to help himself. The means and the reward lay right at hand.

He knotted the pony's reins to the corral's top bar, and straightened. Well pleased with his thoughts, he nodded and a cold smile curved his lips as he started for the house. Good! There was a light in Kerwold's office; and Jane would have gone to bed by now. And that was a good thing, too. What he had to say was between himself and Kerwold; and it would be just as well if there were no one else around.

Without bothering to knock he entered the house, stepped into Kerwold's office and closed the door.

Old Sam looked up with a scowl. "Where the hell you been?"

"Never mind that," Vargas said with a shrug. "I want to talk to you. I've got aplenty to say an' you'd better listen—"

With an oath Old Sam slewed out of his chair, cheeks dark and neck muscles corded. "By God—" he began; but Vargas grinned at him.

"Sit down," he said, "before you fall down."

It was then Sam saw the gun—the sawed-off .44 that was cocked and leveled from Vargas's fist.

"That's better," approved Vargas, chuckling, as Kerwold slumped back in his chair. "Nothin' like a good Colt gun for holdin' a fella's attention." He grinned at Sam wickedly. "Wonder what you'd say if Deef Smith was to learn you been aidin' an' abettin' the outlaw he's been three weeks tryin' to run down? Eh? What would you say if I was to tell him you not only been hidin' Telldane out, but was the fella that got him out here in the first place—the gent that's been hirin' him—"

"I'd say you was a goddam fool an' a liar!"

"Mebbe you would," Vargas grinned, "—but you'd play hell provin' it! On the other hand, I could back up my remarks with concrete evidence—kind of evidence any jury in this land would pass on. I could show Smith that cave Telldane has been holed up in; I could show him the letter I got in my pocket that you sent Bufe, askin' him to come out here—surprises you, don't it? It surprised me, too, when I found it."

When Kerwold could trust himself to speak: "What are you after?" he growled thickly.

"Nothin' but a little land an' a deed from you in writin'," Vargas drawled. "I'm a modest man—you'd be surprised, Sam. All I want is that little jag of pasture above your northwest line camp—up there by that corduroy road."

Kerwold's angry cheeks relaxed a little, showing some of the astonishment he felt. He tipped back his head and looked at his foreman oddly. "What in God's name do you want of *that* land?"

Vargas shrugged. "Just a quit-claim, or some kind of deed to it in writin', Sam. I've got a little money put by. Kind of figured mebbe I'd run me three-four cows an' mebbe a bull or two—"

Kerwold snorted. Then his anger seemed to get the better of him again and he banged a gnarled fist heavily on the desk top. "You damn' coyote! I never been blackmailed in my life—"

"Ssh! Not so loud," interrupted Vargas. "You're not talkin' to Deef Smith—yet." He chuckled silently, like an Indian, at the look on Kerwold's cheeks. Then he said slickly, in a tone as suave as velvet: "No sense usin' ugly words or callin' names in this business; if you want to start in heavin' names I can think of a few myself, an' the jail term for a guy that accessories outlaws . . . Shucks! What's the sense gettin' hot under the collar? You got plenty land—a sight more'n you'll know what to do with, now them Wildcat lands is filed on . . .

"Say!" Vargas exclaimed with suddenly narrowing stare; "Telldane ain't given you a lease on Wildcat, has he?" And, before the rancher could answer: "By God! I b'lieve he has! Well, well! Be kinda tough to go to jail now at last you got what you been fishin' for. Well, there's a way around it. Just git out a pen an'—"

"What's on that land?" Old Sam said, leaning forward.

"You write out that deed an' I'll tell you," Vargas murmured agreeably; but the glitter of his eyes did not change by the slightest fraction. "But you better write it quick—I'm gettin' awful nervous, Sam. I got a bad itch in my trigger finger—"

Abruptly Kerwold chuckled. Leaning back in his chair he crossed his arms and stared at Vargas mockingly. "You been readin' too much Buntline, boy. Go ahead an' yap to Smith—this ain't my signin' night."

The grin fell off Duarte Vargas's face. "What's that?" he gasped, jaw sagging. It was not the smartest of answers, but this unexpected independence had thrown his whole plan off gear.

Kerwold jeered at him, laughed aloud. He said contemptuously: "Go have your talk with Smith. Be amusin' to see how far this pipe dream'll get you—"

"But—but that letter . . ." Vargas faltered. "That letter you wrote Telldane—"

185

"I'll tell Smith it's a forgery—"

"You'll—By God, you'll shout, too!" Vargas struck the desk with a force that shook the room. The fingers of his other hand clamped white about the gun, and his furious face was bloated, was horribly twisted with a wild and raging malevolence. "You'll write that deed an' write it quick, or I'll blow your goddam guts out!"

Kerwold paled but he kept his arms crossed stubbornly.

"Blow ahead," he said; and Vargas shook with anger.

"You goddam fool!" he snarled. "You think I'm scared to kill you? You never been more mistaken in your life!" He thrust his fury-ridden face within short inches of Kerwold's own. "I been away all evenin'—cook'll swear to it. I'll tell Deef Smith I come home an' found Telldane rushin' away from here—I'll say I found you groanin' on the floor, all blood—that you swore Telldane had done it!" His eyes glared at Kerwold balefully. "You goin' to write—"

Whatever else he'd been going to say was lost in gun sound—shattered. He clawed frantically at his chest, spun half around and, mouth sprung wide in a soundless screech, crashed sideways into the desk—slid soggily off it onto the floor.

Through the spraddled fingers of an upthrust arm, Sam Kerwold saw flame belch again from the hip of the man stiff-crouched in the door.

186

And that was all. The world pinched out in a howling black. His body jackknifed from the chair, fell forward in a crumpled heap beside the dead Duarte Vargas.

CHAPTER 23

"—AN' SHE SCREECHIN' LIKE A TOMCAT!"

FOR LONG MOMENTS Telldane stood above Ab Holcomb's body—stood somberly; rooted there by the ugly pattern he had put together from the dead man's words. So many of his preconceived notions had been wrong, had been utterly haywire. He had to fight in those first moments to give Holcomb's story credence. Slowly, then ever more quickly, the picture grew clear and sharpened to a steelpoint focus as the dead man's story threw its light into long-dark corners. It was simple—so bitterly simple. The wonder was that he had not guessed these things before. Every edge of it dovetailed neatly; all the pieces dropped into place—almost all of them anyway.

A little over three years back—just before Telldane had met Jane Kerwold—Gus Pring had come to Holcomb with a proposition. Both men had been Texans, each had known the other by repute; Holcomb had been a rustler, Gus Pring—under another name—had been an absconding West Texas banker. They had, Pring said, considerable in common. It was his suggestion that they combine their spreads and form a syndicate. Holcomb had thought well of the idea, and so the Boxed Double A Cattle Syndicate came into being.

But Holcomb had dealt with too many slippery customers in his time to trust any man very far. Pring might be sincere, but Holcomb was not going to bank on it. He insisted on keeping his property separate and under his own control; but had, under pressure, signed a contract which provided that, in the event either one should chance to die before the other, the surviving partner was to fall heir to the entire combined properties.

About the time Telldane had first met up with Jane Kerwold (near Ballinger, this had been, where the girl had been spending a part of her college vacation with her great uncle Harold) business interests had happened, one day, to take Pring and Holcomb into Ballinger. Pring had met Jane on the street and had been asked to the uncle's house for supper. During the course of that evening Telldane's name had bobbed up frequently and when Pring had suggested a date for the following evening, Jane had expressed her regrets, informing him that she had a previous engagement. Suspecting it was with Telldane, Pring had ascertained the time and, taking Uncle Harold and his wife to see a play-acting troupe to get them out of the way, had left a stage all set for Telldane's special benefit. Pring's melodrama had proved all he could have hoped for. Telldane had arrived at Uncle Harold's to find the woman he was engaged to clasped in the ardent embrace of a tall and florid gentleman togged out in gambler's clothes.

And Telldane—poor fool—had jumped to the hasty and entirely erroneous conclusion it had been intended that he should. Even now his jaw muscles corded as he recalled the leering grin with which the fellow had sped his departure.

Pring had made a fool of him, all right.

Telldane acknowledged it. He'd deserved all Pring had dealt him for the brash, fine-gentleman manner with which he'd waved aside Jane's attempted explanations, declaring that his eyes had already told him all he cared to know of the business. And that very night he'd got out of Texas and had not gone back there since.

Oh, yes, Pring had made a fool of him—but there was going to be an accounting . . .

He forced his mind back to the rest of Holcomb's story. With Telldane thus satisfactorily disposed of, Pring had expected soon to hear the sound of wedding bells. Unaccountably, however, Jane would seem to have turned against him. She'd avoided him for the rest of that summer; and now that she was home again seemed still to be avoiding him, and what times that she couldn't, was casually cool and impersonal.

Pring had been forced to believe at last that Kerwold's Flying K—via wedding bells—was not for him and, without consulting Holcomb, had cast about for other and speedier means of getting his hands on the property. But with Kerwold's visit the other morning and disclosure of the Globe bank deal, all Holcomb's original distrust and suspicion of Pring had been roused again. Little things were remembered; small troubles and minor mysteries assumed their proper perspective—he and Pring had quarreled. Not too bitterly, of course, but enough to set Ab's wits to work. He'd decided Pring needed watching.

But Pring had proved much smarter than Holcomb thought him. Pring had been having Holcomb watched; had learned of Holcomb's activity and had led him into a trap.

Tonight Holcomb, watching Pring's place, had seen the Double Bar Circle boss ride off into the hills and had followed. Pring had gone to a rendezvous with Duarte Vargas, the Kerwold foreman. What they had talked about, Holcomb had been too far off to hear; but the fact that they'd talked, off to themselves this way, had been enough to show him that Pring was up to some more slick work that was not being shared with his partner. Seething with rage and resentment, Holcomb had set out to dog Pring's sign after Pring and Vargas had parted. He had still been following Pring when a rifle, from point blank range, had begun ripping up the echoes. Every shot had struck Holcomb, had swept him from the saddle and left him dying in the trail—he'd been dying, but still was conscious, when Willow Creek Wally rode out of the thicket and jogged off after Gus Pring. After what had seemed to him an endless time, Holcomb had some way managed to catch his horse and climb into the saddle. He had known that he was dying. His thought had been to reach Sam Kerwold and warn him—to foil Gus Pring if it was the last thing he did on earth.

Well, he'd foiled him—or Telldane would.

Telldane examined his sixguns—he was packing two these days—and swung grimly into the saddle. He had lost Jane Kerwold, that was certain. No girl could overlook the things he'd said to her, much less the high-handed way he'd used her. She might forgive, but she could not forget. It was not in human nature to forget such treatment as that. His lack of faith, his intolerant and bigoted certainties, had placed her beyond his reach.

But Pring was not beyond his reach. Pring had sown the wind—let him beware the pending harvest.

Deputy Sheriff Deef Smith was sitting up late; he was at his desk in the two-by-four office

192

darkly brooding over a handful of yellowing dodgers he had dug three weeks ago from his files. The face of Bufe Telldane stared back at him from them—not a good likeness, but good enough. These were old Texas handbills offering rewards for Telldane's apprehension on charges since dismissed. Considering them was heaping coals on the fire of Deef Smith's hatred—a personal animosity he held toward every law-breaker. Undoubtedly Telldane had perpetrated the things described in these dodgers, and just as undoubtedly the things had since been forgiven him by a bunch of soft-headed nitwits in recognition of the man's once-splendid record—as if past virtues excused him!

It always made Smith's blood boil to see an outlaw pardoned. Once an outlaw, always an outlaw! It was Smith's unswervable conviction that the only good outlaws were dead ones; and if he had his way they'd all be dead, or safely caged behind bars.

It was gall and bitter wormwood to him to realize that for three long arduous weeks Bufe Telldane had been laughing at him—at the impotence of Smith's manhunt.

Smith crumpled the dodgers in a savage fist and flung them into a corner. "Goddam fools!" he swore, thinking of the men responsible for Telldane's Texas pardon. "The mealy-mouthed, apron-stringed petticoats! By God, he'll get no pardon here! Just let me get my hands on him! Just—"

It was then he heard the hoofbeats. They brought him grim-lipped out of his chair. And he was that way, one hand reaching for his rifle, when the door was flung open and a white-faced man burst into the room, dust covered, horse lather flecking the knees of his Levi's.

It was the Kerwold cook, Bide Jonathan.

Bide said: "Great Gawd A'mighty, Sheriff! Come out to our place quick! I never in my born—"

"What's up?" Smith's voice rode through the words sharply. He caught Bide Jonathan's shoulder. "Never mind the build-up! What the bloody hell's happened?"

"Murder—coldblooded murder! I swear to Pete, I—"

"I'll swear, too, in a minute! Who's murdered? Who done it?"

"I'm a-tellin' you, ain't I. Telldane—that's who! Come in there like a—"

"*Telldane!* Telldane's *murdered?*" Deef Smith gasped.

"Hell, no! He's murdered Vargas! Vargas an' Kerwold, too, I guess—leastways Sam—"

Wrathful, exasperated, Smith shook the cook without gentleness. "Never mind the frills, you nitwit! Tell me straight out what's happened. When'd it happen? What started it? Tell me all you know about it an' never mind your savin' soul!"

He got the story finally. Telldane, according to Bide Jonathan, had come out to the ranch that evening. Answering Kerwold's hail, Jonathan had entered the old man's office, going on ten o'clock, to find him closeted with Bufe Telldane. They had wanted to see Vargas about something—no, Jonathan didn't know what. Vargas hadn't been round; had left right after supper. After learning this much Kerwold had sent the cook back to his shanty, and a short time later, from that shanty, he had seen Telldane ride off.

"But he musta come back—snuck back, I guess likely, 'cause round eleven o'clock—I'd gone to bed—I heard shots." Springing to the window he had seen that big bay of Lou Safford's—the one Telldane had been riding—hitched before the porch. Alarmed, he'd jumped into his boots and gone pelting for the house. He'd got hardly half across the yard when Telldane came running out. Telldane had seen him, had flung two quick shots at him, vaulted into the saddle and gone hellbending off toward the hills.

Entering the house he'd found a bloody sight awaiting him in Kerwold's office. Vargas lay sprawled in a pool of blood—dead; shot through the back. And across the room Sam Kerwold— all blood, too—had lain, crumpled, beside his overturned chair.

At this point Smith had broken in to ask where Kerwold's daughter was.

"Jane? My savin' soul! Didn't I tell you? Great bulls of Bashan! She was *with* him—with *Telldane.* He come outa that house luggin' her under one arm—an' she screechin' like a tomcat! She was kickin' an' scratchin' an' poundin' him with her helpless little fists—but he was hangin' right onto her like she wasn't no bigger'n a baby—"

"You mean to say he carried her off—"

"I'm tellin' you, ain't I? '*Course* he carried her off—took her up in the hills with him . . ."

Deef Smith didn't hear any more. He wasn't listening. He was busy cramming rifle shells into his pocket. And there was a cold, bright glint in his eye.

CHAPTER 24

APACHES!

IT WAS CLOSE to daylight when Bufe Telldane sighted the headquarters buildings of Pring's Double Bar Circle outfit. In the flat gray haze preceding dawn the place looked gauntly drab, deserted. But Bufe was not dismayed for there were horses in the big corral. His natural inclination was to ride straight over to the house, get Pring out of bed and have it out with him; but natural inclinations, he was beginning to learn, were damned expensive luxuries. Pring was a feud style fighter, deadly as a sidewinder. Twice already Bufe had underestimated the man, and a third time might prove the last. Pring, if he were but half as slick as Holcomb claimed, would not be passing up any bets; he would have considered the possibility of Telldane's coming and have prepared for it.

A creek's twisting course wound a short ways back of the harness shed, and from its eroded lip the ground pitched gently upward toward a low-crowned knoll, or miniature butte that was topped by a stand of timber. Bufe, riding in among those trees, dismounted. He looped the reins of Safford's horse about a juniper's gnarled branch and, easing the marshal's Winchester from beneath the stirrup fender, crept forward to the edge of brush. That vantage afforded him a pretty fair view of the yard below, and he hunkered there on his bootheels with a rifle across his knees, prepared to wait day's coming. If Pring had readied a trap for him, he meant to know it before going down there.

His wind-scoured cheeks were bleakly slanted and the roll of his lips showed bitter—but not one half so bitter as the thoughts that ranged his mind. He watched, but hardly saw the gray yard spread below him; Jane Kerwold's features were before his vision and he could not get them out of it. No pleasant thoughts were these that were tumbling through his head as, with the outward patience of an Indian, he sat watching the false dawn fade from the east. Once he groaned aloud, remembering the words he'd used last night on Jane when by the porch she'd tried to talk with him. He had lost her, irrevocably and finally. By his own acts, by the brutal things he'd said to her, he had scattered the last cold ash of their departed romance.

Day dawned beyond the eastward mountains, the sun's new glory gilding the western bastions, lining with purest gold the faraway peaks of the eastern slopes. Morning came rocking its way across the valley, but nothing stirred in the yard below—nothing human, leastways. The horses in the big corral let out a few desultory whinnies, stretched and peered hungrily across the bars; but that was all.

Telldane watched for another half hour then stiffly rose and climbed into the saddle. He sent the gelding at a slow walk toward the creek, reached it, splashed across, and quartered past the harness shed. Still no sign of movement; nothing to show there were men around.

Odd—uncommon odd.

No smoke came from the cookshack chimney; no sound emanated from the bunkhouse's chinked, log walls. No movement anywhere save that created by the restless broncs in the pole corral.

He got down before the ranch house porch, climbed its steps and crossed its sun-warped planking to pound the butt of his sixgun against the door. Hollow echoes mocked that thumping.

Something was plain enough to Telldane then. Pring was gone. The ranch was deserted.

He stood a moment scowling, then yanked the screen door open and strode inside. Through room after empty room he tramped with scowl growing blacker and blacker. He stood upon the porch again and stared across the yard, bleak gaze roving the horses in the enclosure. Crowbaits. There was not one sound horse there.

Where had Gus Pring gone—and *why?*

What new devilment was the fellow up to that had taken all hands away from this spread? Pring had not quit the country; that much was certain. He had come too close to victory to be pulling a fadeout now; there was no sense to it—no need that Telldane knew of. Pring could not have known that Willow Creek's job was a botched one; it was not likely that Willow Creek himself suspected it. They believed Ab Holcomb dead— as dead as Brill and Ronstadt.

Only one thing could have pulled that outfit away from this spread—more devilment.

Jaw muscles corded, Telldane swung into the saddle. They were some place in this basin and he would find them.

A wild, forbidding stretch of country, this land below the Mogollon Rim; timbered slopes and dust-strewn deserts, a place of lofty peaks and sunken, broiling, rock-choked wastes and gulches. By ten o'clock these flats were stifling and what fitful wind was shouldered off the mesas was furnace-hot. Every bit of metal about Bufe's gear was scorching to the touch and his eyes were red with the glare.

It was in his mind that Pring and his outfit might be trailing stolen Kerwold cattle. Now that Topock was dead, Andy Cooper, he thought, might have cast his lot with Pring; for certainly

Pring would have been cognizant of their activities. It was in the cards he might have made a deal with Cooper just as he had with Willow Creek Wally and—yes, as quite probably he had with Vargas. All along, ever since first meeting the man that night when he'd come from the trees by the corduroy road, Telldane had felt Duarte Vargas was playing a double game. Kerwold had scoffed at the notion, but Kerwold's enemies were out to smash him, and where could an agent of those enemies be better placed than right in Kerwold's outfit?

He left off thinking abruptly, narrowed eyes intently staring, body stiffened in the saddle. From the tip of Humbolt Mountain, far ahead to the north, a smoke was rising straight into the sky; and Bufe's raking glance flashing eastward across the hazed horizon found others. Saddle Mountain—Cypress Peak—Four Peaks Mountain—Sugarloaf! From each of those crests smoke thrust its gray tail into the sky; and Telldane was seized with a sudden conviction. Someone was keeping tabs on him, signaling his whereabouts, smoke-talking about his progress and direction!

He reined up with cheeks gone sober. It would hardly be Pring who was so interested in his actions, for every contact he had had with the man had advertised Pring's opinion. Pring was not only unafraid of Telldane; he was contemptuous of him. Having framed him so neatly once, the boss of Double Bar Circle would surely never consider it necessary to camp all these scouts on Bufe's trail.

It was a time for thought and Bufe thought hard. And the upshot of that thinking was remembrance of the deputy—Deef Smith. Bufe's dust-streaked face flicked a twisted grin. Yes, that would be Smith. The man had spent three bitter weeks savagely casting for Telldane's sign, trying to run Telldane to earth. The futility of those efforts must have pricked the deputy's ego like the stabs of a Spanish dagger. Deef Smith—in Smith's opinion—was no safe man to trifle with; and Bufe, knowing something of the lawman's reputation, could see how Deef Smith would be wild to get him. He had thought the man would have given up, but it was plain now that he hadn't.

And then Bufe's roving glance crossed something that sprang his eyes wide open; and he leaned forward, startled, amazedly staring at the ground. There in the dust of the trail before him was a track. A moccasin track—the clear-cut shape of a buckskin-covered foot!

Apaches!

There was no doubt in Bufe's active mind as to the meaning of those smokes now. Deef Smith, determined to get him, was employing Apache scouts!

Even as the realization clutched him the hot sand bulged beside the track, dust geysered suddenly from it and the sharp flat crack of a rifle kicked across the stifling silence.

Telldane's spurs flashed wickedly. Safford's horse lunged forward with a rushed, hip-jolting violence and settled to a flogging run with Telldane, riding Indian fashion, hanging on by a knee and an arm.

CHAPTER 25

"You Can Cross Telldane Off the Books!"

JANE KERWOLD, following Bufe Telldane's departure, did not go at once to bed. Reentering the house and retiring to the privacy of her room, she sat for a long time by the window thinking. She sat with dark blue eyes, widely wistful, regarding the play of light and shadow, watching it build and break its patterns in the empty yard outside. Like life those patterns were, she thought; and sighed now and again as wind whipped lonely anthems from the dusty foliage of the trees.

She saw Duarte Vargas by the moon's cool light ride into the yard and leave his horse by the big corral. She wondered idly where he'd been then heard his step upon the porch, heard the screen door close behind him, and found herself reflecting this was the first time she could remember that he had not let it slam.

Some fifteen minutes later another horse came into the yard—came so quietly that it was there in the cottonwoods' shadows before she became

204

aware of it; and even then she was not sure until it crossed a patch of moonlight and she saw it plainly, briefly, and recognized its rider.

Gus Pring.

It looked like Gus. The man had Gus's way of sitting a saddle.

Again she sighed, and hoped she was no part of whatever reason had brought him here at this late hour. And that was queer, when she stopped to think of it, for there had been a time when knowledge of Gus's presence would have been a welcome thing—indeed it *had* been, many times. But that had been before she'd met grim, taciturn Bufe Telldane.

She was still there by the window, absorbed with thoughts of Bufe Telldane, when gun sound jerked her from the chair. Jerked her upright, frightened, trembling, startled eyes fixed on the door. She sprang toward it, wrenched it open, went down the hall in quick alarm.

For a moment, coming in from the dark, the light in Kerwold's office blinded her; and then, turned sick with horror, sight returned and the room in ghastly focus sprang clear before her eyes. There lay Vargas in grotesque posture, glazed eyes staring, beside the desk. His twisted mouth hung open; blood was bright upon his shirt. And there, just beyond, face down, was sprawled her father; and above him, smoking pistol still in hand, was crouched Gus Pring.

"Gus!"

The choked cry spun Pring round.

Jane screamed when she saw the look of him. With blazing eyes, he sprang for her. Terrified, Jane whirled, tried to reach the hall. But he was too quick for her. She tripped, was falling when she felt herself yanked backward, felt his arms close round her. A rough hand then cut short her screams and everything went black.

She was jarred awake by an agonizing sense of movement. Every tortured muscle ached, her nerves were screaming and her wrists and ankles felt as though they were being cut in two. Her jerked-open eyes found a world still dark; a creaking, thumping, jangling world that would not hold still for a second. Then awareness came that she was on a horse, was tied face down across a saddle; her wrists and ankles were tightly lashed beneath the animal's belly.

Consciousness must have left her then, for next time she opened her eyes things seemed lighter, a sort of leprous gray color as though mist-blotched and barnacled. All her weight was against the cantle and her wrists and ankles felt as though they were about to be twisted off of her. The horrible, blinding pain of it all was enough to make her faint. But she did not faint; not then, at least. And, presently, her reeling senses discovered that the horse was climbing a hill. Gravity it was that kept her weight so hard against the cantle. Perhaps it was gravity that made her head throb so; seemed as though in another moment it must surely burst. As something to get her mind off it she tried to identify her surroundings. But hanging butchered-steer fashion, head down from a saddle, was not conducive to great feats of observation. All she could see through the swirling dust were occasional patches of sand and sliding rubble.

But she was not alone. That much was plain. There was a deal too much noise—not to mention the dust, to be made by one lone horse.

She tried to cry out, to attract attention. But couldn't. There was a lump in her mouth and her cramped tongue was dry as cotton. She tried to waggle it round. The strange lump gave a little, soggily; but it would not go away and she could not—though she tried—spit it out. It came to her then what it was. It was cloth—she was gagged!

Trussed up and gagged, lashed fast to somebody's saddle!

It was not the sort of knowledge from which great comforts are taken. She must be a prisoner—a captive possibly, or hostage. The knowledge was not conducive to any tremendous satisfaction, either. While she was pondering it, remembrance came with all its resurrected horror. The recollections overwhelmed her.

When her reeling senses became again cognizant of the things immediately about her, the jar of motion seemed to have stopped. Her limbs were numb and useless and her head was a blinding torture. Through the pulsing, throbbing agony of it came knowledge of another's presence close by. No—that was wrong; there must be *several* men about her. She could hear their grumbling voices. Then someone was cutting her ropes away. Someone else lifted her out of the saddle; but when they set her down she crumpled miserably in a heap. Her legs—coming back to life—stung as though skewered by hatpins; but they would not hold her up—not even with the aid of the big rough hand that, viselike, gripped her shoulder. They buckled again, futilely, and somebody close by swore.

Then a lantern abruptly was thrust in her face, and by its flare she saw the lower half of one side of a vest, a dark, indiscriminate patch of shirt, the flaring wings of bullhide chaps; but of their wearer's face she saw nothing at all. The lantern light did not strike it.

Then a voice said gruffly: "Bring her along," and another voice said maliciously: "I'd give somethin' to see Telldane's mug when he finds out this dame is missin'!"

Cooper's voice, that last. She was certain.

The first speaker laughed. "Prob'ly won't be hearin' about it—I've an idea he's goin' to be

208

busy. The cook's been greased an' he's gone to town with a tale for Deef Smith's ear. Unless Smith's changed, you can cross Telldane off the books."

CHAPTER 26

COOPER LAYS PIPE

COOPER had not, as Topock had supposed, killed Ronstadt, the Buck Basin homesteader. But Cooper had been well suited to let his erstwhile pardner believe he had; that belief had eliminated possibly embarrassing questions. As a matter of fact, it had been Vargas who had killed Juke Ronstadt. Cooper had seen him do it and had determined to find out why. And he had, at last, but it had not been easy. Vargas was a canny customer with an ingrained habit of caution. That habit, on Cooper's part, had occasioned a good many oaths. Indirectly it had brought about Vargas's death; for had Kerwold's doublecrossing foreman not been attempting to make doubly sure a matter already certain, he would not have been round at the time of Pring's visit and would have been, therefore, quite probably still numbered among the quick.

But Cooper was satisfied to have him out of the way; he had learned why the man had killed Ronstadt. The knowledge was not an unmixed blessing, and he'd shared it for quite some time.

Ronstadt had been killed because, inadvertently, he had stumbled across a secret—Vargas's secret; and now Mr. Cooper had discovered it, with all its attendant risks and worries. And the risks were there, and the worries, too. For the substance of Duarte Vargas's secret was cached on Kerwold land.

It was this knowledge that finally had swung Cooper over to Pring. He had early sensed that the Double Bar Circle boss was far from the disinterested spectator that he would have other folks believe. Cooper had watched Gus Pring as he'd watched Duarte Vargas, patiently and assiduously; and the watching had borne fruit. Vargas was mixed in the valley's turbulence in the hope of grabbing onto that precious find; a something Vargas wanted but had not the guts to file on while Sam Kerwold lived to exact vengeance. But Gus Pring's purpose in smashing Kerwold was of larger, more far-seeing scope; this basin was a paradise for cow raisers—a veritable cattle empire, but Gus Pring could not grab it so long as Kerwold lived and prospered. Therefore, both to Pring and to Vargas, as Cooper saw it, Sam Kerwold was a barrier, an obstruction to be removed.

To Cooper, the removal of all three of these hombres was a prime and urgent necessity. But first, he'd told himself, give Pring and Vargas rope—give them all the rope they wanted; and after that . . . his turn would come.

And now that turn was coming.

Cooper, knowing it, chuckled. For *he'd* ambition, also. His craving for power and opulence had been as great as any man's. Nor was he averse to a good-looking wife.

His recipe was comprehensive.

And it was working—oh, so beautifully!

Already Sam Kerwold was out of the saddle, murdered last night by Gus Pring. Ab Holcomb and other lesser lights—they'd been taken care of, too. There was not a homesteader left in the country. Except Telldane, of course, who had filed on Wildcat. And *he'd* not be around long. Pring, slick fellow, had framed Telldane for Kerwold's murder, and that guy, Deef Smith, would finish him. Telldane, once, had risen from the dead; but he'd pull no rise act this time! And Vargas was dead, and his secret safe; and as for calico—Well, Cooper had kind of taken a shine to Jane Kerwold. And here she was, put right in his hands by Pring, locked up in that yonder cabin.

Again Cooper chuckled. Things were shaping up pretty nice—pretty damned nice! There was only one fly in the ointment—Pring himself; and maybe . . .

He took Willow Creek Wally aside, well out of the other boys' hearing. "Well?" Willow Creek eyed him wonderingly.

"No," Cooper said, "it ain't. In fact, I don't

mind tellin' you it's pretty damn bad. I don't like the look of things at all."

"What you mean, don't like the look of 'em?"

"Just that. All this killin' an' girl-snatchin'!"

Willow Creek shrugged. "No skin off my nose—yours either. Gus Pring's the one that's done it. An' you got to hand it to him—"

"You sure have," Cooper said dryly. "He's slicker'n slobbers—"

"What's up your sleeve?" Willow Creek said. "What you drivin' at?"

"Ain't sure I know myself, but I'm gettin' goddam suspicious. I dunno what he's got in mind for me, but he's sure as hell got you down for a first-class necktie party."

Willow Creek's face showed the hoped-for reaction; his growl was a proper-pitched sound. "By God, if you—"

"Shh! you fool! Not so loud," Cooper snarled, with a quick glance across at the men. "It may be I'm wrong. I hope I am, but—Well, it's this way, Wally. I overheard Gus tellin' off a couple boys to swear your neck into hemp. They're to push the word around that you an' Telldane is pardners—"

"Pardners!" Willow Creek exploded. "*Me* an' *Bufe Telldane?* Why—"

"I know—I know," Cooper cut in suavely, "but that don't make no never-mind. The idea is for these two fellas—soon's Smith's got Telldane's light blown out—to come forward an' swear they seen you waitin' for Bufe in the timber last night; that when you parted he went one way an' you, takin' the girl, went another. Fixes it pretty neat, don't it, why Telldane ain't got the girl he's s'posed to've run off with?" He showed a sympathy for Willow Creek's emotion, adding pointedly: "It also gets you out of the way for when it's time to count up the profits. 'Course, I may be mistaken, you know. *Mebbe* I misunderstood what I heard; but I figured you'd ought to know about it."

CHAPTER 27

LOST TIMBERS

WHEN BUFE TELLDANE again swung upright in the saddle he was a good many miles from where the unknown marksman had let drive at him with a rifle from the rimrock. He'd cleared out of that place in a hurry, but his mind had not been idle. The chances were it was one of Deef Smith's Indians who had cut loose at him back there. But it might have been the deputy himself and Bufe wasn't taking any chances. For the time being, at any rate, he aimed to put himself out of reach. Time enough to get on Pring's trail after Smith had been shaken off his own trail.

So he headed for the Verde River.

He rode hard and fast, and when he reached the broken ground along it he sent Safford's horse between red bluffs and went angling down a wash that took him into the bottoms and along these, skirting the river, he rode north at an easier pace. Deef Smith's scouts, so long as he kept below the rim, would have considerable difficulty keeping track of his progress.

He stopped at noon in a kind of cove, unsaddled

and staked his horse to graze. In the shade of a desert willow he lay down and drowsed for two or three hours; after which, with a smoke between his lips, he considered the situation.

Had something new happened to cause Deef Smith to get those Apaches after him? Or was it accumulated gall and spite on the deputy's part that had brought him to their hire? Smith was a go-getter; it was both his record and his boast. He had a reputation for getting his man and it was plain he aimed to get Bufe. So far as Telldane had ever heard, Deef Smith was honest, played a straight game. No holds were barred when he got on the trail, but he didn't go out of his way to hound a man just because a man had a bad name.

Smith must, therefore, believe that Telldane had murdered Brill. He must believe Telldane had shot and killed Safford because Safford had gotten the goods on him with regard to Brill's killing. Still and all, in the three weeks Smith had been hunting him he had not before employed Indians.

Telldane considered this, grimly thoughtful.

He considered some other things as well. He considered, for instance, Ab Holcomb and Holcomb's story; he considered Duarte Vargas and Pecos Gann. Holcomb, of course, had known him at once—as soon as he'd first laid eyes on him; for Telldane had been the reason for Holcomb's migration from Texas where Ab had been doing a profitable business rustling other people's steers. Telldane had been a stock detective then and had let Holcomb get away; in fact, he had warned the man he had *better* haul freight if he put any value on freedom. There was a chance, he had thought, Holcomb might go straight . . . The point was, Holcomb—when Bufe had come into this basin—had known him. It was Telldane's belief that Gann and Vargas had also known him, or had pretty well guessed who he was. There was, contributory to this notion, that scene in Ransome's store on the night of Bufe's arrival when Pecos Gann, crying "Jeez! D'you know—" had jumped a blurred hand for his gun.

Yes, it seemed pretty certain that Gann and Vargas had known him. It had been Vargas, riding out of the trees, who'd suggested his going to the store. Vargas must have known that Sam had written Bufe . . . Each must have feared Bufe's coming—but why?

True, Gann had been mixed up with Topock—might even have been taking pay from Pring. But Vargas . . . Where did Kerwold's foreman come in? Had he, like others in this basin, been working all along for Pring? Holcomb had said last night he'd trailed Gus Pring to a rendezvous with Vargas . . .

Telldane gave it up for the time. The whole damn thing was so mixed up, it made him dizzy to think of it. For one reason or another practically every man of importance in this country was out to down Sam Kerwold. All of them were Kerwold's enemies, which was all Bufe needed to know. Their various motives weren't important. It *was* important to see that their schemes bore no fruit. That was why Kerwold had got him here.

Bufe picked up his rifle and prowled along the bottoms, finally rousting out a jackrabbit which he shot and promptly cleaned. Building a tiny fire then, he cooked and ate it. And then took another nap.

It was dark when he woke up.

He saddled Safford's horse and rode north along the river in the direction of distant Ashfork. When he reached the big bend east of Saint Clair Mountain, he climbed up out of the bottoms and took the road from Davenport Wash and followed it leisurely southwest till it reached Camp Creek. Hoof sound, then, drove him off the trail. With a clamping hand across the gelding's nostrils, he waited in the brush by its side.

There were six riders in the party; two whites and four breech-clouted bucks. They weren't picking any posies, either, but despite the speed with which they passed Bufe's covert, the moonlight showed him Deef Smith's face, and its expression made him glad he'd wheeled from the trail. They were hunting him, no doubt of that!

He waited another ten minutes and was just swinging into the trail when he heard them coming back again—leastways, someone was coming—several someones, by the sound. What had happened? Not that it made much difference. He could see what would happen all right if they caught sight of him.

He put Safford's horse into the creek's dry bed and quietly eased him south. It did not take him long, however, to realize the futility of quiet. Smith's crowd had stopped back there in the trail; tiny bursts of light suggested they were striking matches, and he remembered then the flattened calk on the off rear shoe of Safford's horse.

He abandoned quiet and spurred for speed. This was no time for stealth or parley. Contact with Smith and those Indians with him could have but one result—gunplay. There'd been too much of that already.

Coming out of the creek bed half an hour later, he cut through the timber for higher ground. Smith's crowd, like hell emigrating on cartwheels, was coming fast, not far behind.

Telldane pulled up on a little knoll, keening the southflung reaches spread below in the moon's pale light. Yonder line was Kerwold's ripped-up fence. Off there was Wildcat Hill. Smith's bunch, by the sound, had reached the place where he'd left the creek—were making quite a commotion. He could hear Smith's voice, keyed tight with rage, snapping commands like a whiplash. He was spreading them out, going to beat the timber.

Bufe's glance swept the shadows with a risen vigilance as he kneed Safford's horse off the knoll. He sent it quietly downward, angling toward the demolished line fence, veering sharply back into the timber when he realized that boundary's lack of cover.

A challenge slammed after him through the gloom.

"You, over there, headin' west! Who are you? Sing out, goddam—"

Telldane sank his spurs. The gelding lunged for the open. A rifle cracked through the hoof-pound sharply, twice. The first shot withered past Telldane on the left; the second kicked splintered bark from a tree bole just ahead of him, and then all the rifles back of him let go in a solid blast of sound. A branch above his head cracked off. With twigs falling all around him Telldane put his bronc across the fence. Three long jumps it made, and staggered. The horse was done. Bufe left the saddle—lit on braking bootheels, skidded, and went plunging for a clump of young elder with the whine of lead tearing whistles of sound all about him.

Across his shoulder as he crashed through the thicket, Wildcat Hill reared bleakly black against the northwest stars. The base of that long slope was bathed in moonlight, devoid of cover. That way was out; he must go some other. His raking glance zigzagged the shadows. Straight west, south of and paralleling the torn-up fence, was a scrub oak stand, its pooled gloom promising the only shelter he could see.

Pistol in hand he lunged from the thicket, low-crouched, heart pumping fiercely. They hadn't seen him; the elder thicket cut off their view— they were still tunneling it with their lead, their noise drowning out the sound of his running.

He was almost into the scrub oak stand when a man's voice bit from its shadows.

"Hold it!"

Telldane, gathering his muscles, sprang. Not aside, but straight ahead, straight at the point where the voice had come from. He had to get into that scrub oak or die. A gun's flame burst in his face as the momentum of his drive brought him square against the hidden man, carrying him backward, shoulder hard against the fellow's chest. The gun went off again, that flash of light showing Willow Creek's face. Then they were down in a tangle of thrashing arms and legs. Shock hammered Telldane's ribs to the muffled explosion of Willow Creek's gun; then his own gun barrel struck Willow Creek's head and the man went limp as a meal sack.

Breathing hard, Bufe reached his feet. A back-flung glance showed Smith's bunch breaking from the elder. He hammered two shots, heard a man's strangled yell and, without waiting to see more, dashed west through the trees.

Five minutes' hard running brought him to their edge. He pulled up, trying to throttle his labored breathing to hear if they were coming. They were.

Dead ahead, beyond the fringe of trees, lay the corduroy road. Here was where he'd met Duarte Vargas the night he had come into this country.

The rotten timbers of that road would leave no track—very little sound. He moved onto it, still running, and struck south. Its course was angling. The old road curled and twisted through the trees. Back of him Deef Smith's riders left the oak; they'd not know which way he'd gone—would have to spread out.

Bufe left the road, swinging east. The brush grew thicker, impeding progress, making stealth impossible. He was cursing his luck when something tripped him, hurled him heavily through the brush. The ground gave way beneath his weight and dropped him, rolling, frantically clawing, sharply downward. He stopped suddenly, brought up in a choking cloud of dust.

It was dark—pitch dark, and he'd lost his gun. He sat cat-still, intently listening. Sound of the posse reached him dimly, became vaguer with distance and finally quiet.

He got to his feet then, striking a match. His glance, whipped around, sprang suddenly wide. The walls of this hole were of rotten timber. Man-laid timber—he was in a shaft! The shaft of some old, long-forgotten mine!

In the east wall a tunnel led off into Stygian gloom. And there as its mouth, aglint in the light, lay his pistol. He stooped to retrieve it, went still with an oath. The dust was laced with the tracks of boots, and not all of them old ones—not by a jugful!

He picked up his gun and went into the tunnel. He dropped his match and struck another, coming presently to where some recent working had widened the passage. Against the near wall was a pick and a powder keg; the opposite wall was piled high with filled sacks. He examined the side where the pick had been used and soundlessly whistled beneath his breath.

He saw the answer to several things now—saw plainly what Duarte Vargas had been doing up there by the road the night he'd arrived—Vargas had probably just left this place. Kerwold's foreman had apparently found what its owners had given up searching for. Gold! That whole blame wall was lousy with it!

Bufe had just made this discovery when voice sound grabbed him, pulled him upright.

Deef Smith was coming back.

CHAPTER 28

Skull Mesa

THE CREAK of saddle gear, the jingle and clank of spur and bridle chains, drew nearer and stopped. Telldane, stiff-crouched in the tunnel, could hear quite plainly the savage growl of Deef Smith's voice. They must, he thought, be halted some place almighty close to the shaft top.

Deef Smith was laying the law down. "Makes no damn diff'rence!" he snapped. "Unless he's growed wings he's hid out around here somewheres, an' by grab he'll stay bottled up here till I can git men enough to roust him out! Keeler, you take these bucks an' string 'em out where they can watch this whole smear of country. There'll be a thousan' bucks in it, hard money, for the gent that brings him down. Now git on an'— Never mind that! I'm goin' to poke around some more over to Kerwold's—might find somethin' that cook overlooked . . . You told Ed Cranton to get them bodies, didn't you?"

That was all Bufe heard just then; he was too startled by the implication in Deef Smith's reference to Cranton to bother with the rest of

224

it. Cranton was the Ashfork undertaker—what bodies was he supposed to have been told about? Telldane did not care for that talk of bodies—not even a little bit. Something had been happening; a whole and ornery lot by the sound, and . . .

He pulled up again, listening. The sound of hoofs was dying out, being swallowed up by distance as the scouts moved off, again to take up their vigil. They—but all of them weren't gone! There was horse sound right above him now!

Bufe made his mind up pronto.

This tunnel must lead out of here . . .

It did. Parting a mesquite's branches he saw the shine of stars again; and there on a crest by the old timbered road, sharp-cut against the moonglare, showed the stiff, cocked shape of a horseman—*Smith!*

Deef Smith it certainly was. Equally obvious was the fact that Smith, with that rifle across his knees, was lingering in the hope that his quarry, thinking him departed with the rest, would come catfooting from his hideout. What Smith meant to do in that case was plain as paint on a pot lid!

Smith was less than twenty yards off and was facing the other way. But he faced round quick enough when a voice said softly: "Grab a cloud an' hang onto it, hombre." He faced round with an oath, gun lifted to shoot—but there was nothing in sight for a target.

Telldane said: "I'll not ask again," and, cursing, Smith put his hands up.

"Let go of that gun an' ride straight south—ride *slow!* That's fine. Pull up."

Telldane stepped out of the branches, six-shooter cocked and leveled. "Slide down, an' do it careful. I'd just as lief shoot as not," he said. "Now tie that nag so he won't wander off." And, when Smith had done so, Telldane relieved him of his belted gun and prodded him through the branches.

"What the hell is this—"

"Tunnel," Bufe said succinctly. "Strike a match an' lead the way."

"You goddam fool!" Smith snarled. "You'll never cut it! I've got—"

"Just let me worry about that. Get movin'!"

When they reached the wide place where the sacks were piled, Bufe said: "There's a candle stump. Light it—that's fine. Now sit down an' get the weight off your heels. Whose bodies was Cranton supposed to get?"

Smith was staring round curiously.

"Vargas's secret mine," Bufe said. "C'mon now, answer my question."

"Whose bodies," Smith mocked: "that's rich, that is! You lousy back-shootin' killer! Where've you got that girl?"

"What girl?"

"Jane Kerwol—*Hey!*"

226

Telldane took his grip from Smith's throat and stepped back, cheeks white, eyes blazing. His voice was bleak, repressed, hard-held. "Talk," he said, "and talk fast!"

Smith did. Sullenly, with lips peeled back, he told the story Kerwold's cook had brought him; told how he'd gone to the Flying K, of what he'd found when he got there. "I suppose," he sneered when he finished, "you'll tell me somebody's framed you."

Telldane told him nothing of the kind. "I've got to borrow your horse—"

"You crazy loon! You can't git away! I've—"

"I've no intention of getting away. I'm goin' after that girl," Bufe said coldly. "Peel off that belt and put your hands behi—"

"Like h—" Smith's bluster died at the look of Telldane's face; he grudgingly did as ordered. "But you—"

"For your information," Bufe cut in, "it's Pring that's behind all this—wake up an' get your eyes open! It's Pring that's got Jane Kerwold, too— the man's hog-wild for power! Gone to his head; he's tryin' to grab this entire valley. The fool's gone mad as a hatter! For God's sake, use your head, Smith! Can't you *see* it?"

"I can see you swingin' at a rope!" Smith snarled; but Bufe paid no attention.

"He's bribed Sam's cook, that's plain enough— probably killed him by now to shut his mouth. It's a cinch he knows about this mine—that's why he killed Vargas; one of his reasons anyway. Pretty slick of him framin' me for Sam's murder—but he's pulled that trick once too often."

Bufe paused, then added grimly: "Look here, Smith; you ought to be able to see this much—"

"I can see your face when they kick the trap out from under you!" Smith jeered. "You might's well surrender now an' save yourself some trouble. You'll never get—"

"Listen, you damn fool!" Telldane gritted. "Can't you see what's goin' to happen to that girl? She must have seen him—recognized him; elseways, why would he have carried her off? Do you think you'll ever see her again? You won't if I can't stop him! He—"

But Smith was grinning at him sourly. "'F I had your talkin' talents—"

Bufe saw there was no use arguing with him; nothing could change him. He was convinced of Telldane's guilt and would consider no alternative. Bufe dared waste no further time. He tied Smith up and left him. He knew the man would get loose of that belt, but it would serve till Bufe got clear.

Well, Pring had bested him again—but he'd not have long to brag of it! Meantime, Bufe must ride; and fast. There was one slender chance Jane was still alive . . .

● ● ●

Telldane knew that soon as he struck open country Smith's Apache scouts would spot him; and they did. Rifles opened up from the rimrock and the scream of lead was all about him. Crouched low above Smith's saddle he urged the game horse on with quirt and spur; and, ears laid flat, it flew like a rocket, straight out from under the Indian guns, a silver streak in the moonlight. But one chance shot, or a gopher hole, Bufe knew, would send them crashing, and he prayed for luck as much as for speed; he would need luck this night—plenty of it.

The Indian yells dimmed out behind; the crack of Indian rifles. But these would follow—even now, Bufe guessed, Smith's scouts would be catching up horses. And Smith himself, directed by those shots, would soon be dogging the trail. But that was all right. Let him keep his lead and the whole damn country could follow! What he aimed to do would not take long—just the time for squeezing a trigger. After that they could have him, he guessed; he hadn't very much to live for.

For he was not fooled. Knowledge—that knowledge recently acquired from Holcomb— that Jane had not been the capricious, perfidious cheat he had supposed, did not excuse the supposition. He had thought her one and called her one—only last night he had said to her face, things no woman could ever excuse. No, those

229

fond hopes were done with—as dead as they'd been three years ago—deader; blasted by scorn and mockery, destroyed by lack of faith. But, even if they hadn't been, the knowledge of his turbulent years, of the things he'd done in this valley, would have driven her from him in repugnance. Proclaimed an outlaw from Usery Pass to the Limestone Hills, Telldane's future was sealed—sealed with blood and dishonor; tied with calumny, like the rope Smith would put round his neck.

But before they closed the books on him, there was one more chore for his guns. If he could, he must save Jane Kerwold and send Gus Pring to hell.

From time to time backward looks were flung across his shoulder, and each time his head twisted front again, his mouth showed tighter, more cracklike.

They were coming all right. Smith and his yelling Indians were not a mile behind him; not gaining, thank God! but holding even, holding the pace like hounds. One false step on his bronc's part though—

He prayed—and prayed again. Not for greater speed but for his horse's safe arrival at the ranch atop Skull Mesa. And Bufe prayed thoroughly; not with lips alone, but with soul and heart—with every last energy in him.

For he was sure that Gann's gutted ranch, or its vicinity, was where Pring had taken Jane. Obviously Gann, all along and unknown to Ab Holcomb, had been working in Gus Pring's interests. It was the only explanation that would fit Gann into things. He had, of course, allowed Cooper and Topock to use his place as a relay stop in their stealing of Kerwold's cattle; but Bufe greatly doubted if Topock or Cooper, either, had yet taken a cent of profit. Gus Pring would have seen to that; they'd have been stalled off with some fancy tale—slick talking was Gus Pring's strong point. But now that Pring's game was cut-and-run, what better place could he run to? what place was less apt of suspicion? He would keep out of reach till Telldane was done, till something happened to Smith.

It was after midnight when Bufe sighted Gann's gutted buildings. He did not stop but slewed a circle round them and cut for Gann's north line camp. That place, he knew, was still intact. There was a tank there and a tumbledown shack, a horse corral and cattle pens; and there—God granting him luck—he would find Jane Kerwold, a prisoner.

Then, as the breakneck pace of Smith's roan gelding whipped him across a ridge, he saw it—a dark, devil's pattern of upthrust blocks against the mouth of a draw. Saw the horses—six of them, saddled and hitched by the big corral.

Clickety clack, clickety clack. The wind-brought sound of the clattering mill was abruptly stilled, lost and flattened in the pounding crash of exploding guns. Flame blossomed from the cabin wall in lurid streaks. The rip and thump of lead—the whine of its passing, was a risen wail in Telldane's brain as, low across the roan's stretched neck, he spurred straight on without pausing or swerving.

Smith's horse was used to the screech of lead and, with ears laid back, it gave all it had.

Two hundred, one-fifty—eighty yards; that near they had gotten when Bufe jerked the rifle from under his leg and drove its last shot at the huddle of horses. Like a dynamited hill that group split apart. One reared straight up and fell backwards screaming; two more were down in thrashing heaps—a fourth was pitching. The final pair broke anchorage, took the top bar with them. From the cabin door two men lunged toward them.

Bufe dropped the rifle and snatched out a pistol. Three times its fanning hammer fell. One man's white face twisted clear around. Plain in the moonlight. Willow Creek Wally. He went toppling backward like a pole-axed steer.

The other man made a saddle—slashed wildly with a ten-inch blade at the reins still tied to the dragging bar. He had nearly cut them when Bufe's shot took him, smashing him slanchways from the squealing bronc.

But this was passing turmoil. Bufe had not stopped. Smith's horse still was carrying him straight for the cabin. Guns winked light from door and window; but panic, desperation, had unsteadied their aim. He was twenty yards off when they scored their hit. They must have fired together. A deafening blast rocked across the yard. Bufe felt it strike. Its travel came up the gelding's legs.

The horse was going. Bufe kicked free of the stirrups as its head went down. The uprearing saddle hurled him forward. He struck on his chest and plowed five feet through choking dust. He came out of it on one knee and an elbow, the pistol still savagely clenched in his fist. There were two shots left. He used them, drove them both at the dark crouched shape that bulked in the door—saw it fall.

The flash of his gun briefly lit the cabin. The sight inside sent his heart to his boots; hung him breathless and frozen, just short of the door.

There were two men inside—two men and Jane Kerwold; those exploding shells had shown her face, chalk white, twisted toward him from where she struggled in the grip of Pring's arm. But Pring had her fast and was safe behind her; he laughed as his free hand brought up a gun— laughed deeply, exultantly, triumphant and mocking. "Go on," he jeered, "shoot!"

And somebody did—but it wasn't Telldane.

233

It was Cooper.

His shape showed, crouched, across the room. Bufe saw the leaping flame that left it. He was to the side of, slightly back of, Pring; and his shot took the rancher beneath the left arm where his clutch of the girl exposed his ribs. Jane fell free as he staggered back; and a swift lunge took Bufe through the door in a long, low dive that ended at Cooper. Cooper's shot ripped its track across Bufe's cheek. Then Bufe's arms locked hard round Cooper's legs and carried him crashing against the wall.

The gun went skittering from Cooper's grasp. Bufe's own, shot empty, had been dropped before he sprang. But Cooper had a knife and meant to use it. Bufe caught the glint of it just in time and flung himself backward.

Rage ripped from Cooper in a snarl of breath. In the powder-fumed murk he was just a black shape, but Rufe saw it coming and again lurched aside. The blade thwunked wickedly into the wall. Before Cooper could jerk it free, a voice snapped harshly: "Hold it! First guy moves gets tunneled!" and a match burst redly from the pooled gloom of the doorway.

It threw weird light across and showed Cooper crouched and glaring; showed Deef Smith well into the room with a six-shooter gripped in each fist and the look on his face a dire warning. Showed the crowded bucks stolid-cheeked round

234

the door, every man of them packing a rifle. The man with the match lit a lamp on the wall and shifted his rifle suggestively.

"All right, Cooper," Smith said. "Get away from that knife. I've got him covered—"

"Got *him* covered!" Jane cried hysterically. "You'd better cover *Cooper!*"

Smith's eyes raked her briefly, returned to the scowling Cooper. "Why should I cover Cooper?"

"Because," Jane cried, "he was Pring's chief gun boss—it was Pring that's been back of all this—"

"Now that's damn foolishness," Smith growled testily. "I know you're upset an' all that—willin' to make allowance for it. But it's Bufe Telldane that's behind this trouble, an'll swing for it, too, by godfreys!" He said to Cooper: "Who killed Gus?"

A crafty look edged Cooper's cheeks. An outflung arm pointed square at Telldane. "Him—the goddam loafer wolf!"

"That's a lie!" Jane blazed. "Don't let him wriggle clear of this," she said, flinging round on Smith.

"What's she talkin' about?" Cooper snapped, with a show of surprised resentment. "You'd think we hadn't saved her, t' listen to her yap—"

"Don't you dare stand there and lie—it won't do you a bit of good now, anyway." She said to Smith: "I've got the cook's signed statement—

235

got it right here in my blouse. Bufe hadn't a thing to do with those murders, or with my being here, either. He saw what you hadn't the *wit* to see and came over here trying to rescue me—and he's done it, too! The man you—"

"Hell, I heard enough o' this!" Cooper snarled, starting for the door.

"Just a minute," said Deef Smith softly. "I think we'll look into this—keep him covered, boys." And, to Jane: "You say Gus Pring—"

"Of course!" Jane said more calmly: "Gus was trying to grab this basin and I think my father caught onto him. At any rate—" And she told Deef Smith the story; all of it that she knew; about going into the office last night and finding Pring, gun in hand. "He bribed the cook to ride in and tell you those lies," she said; "and afterwards, when the cook joined us here, Gus killed him—but he didn't die right off; he managed to give me a paper, and it tells the truth!"

She started toward Bufe, but Smith's arm stopped her. "Hold still a bit. I want to get this straight in my mind. You say Gus Pring killed your father and Vargas? that Cooper here's been workin' for Gus—"

"Yes, and so was Vargas and Willow Creek, who used to be Holcomb's range boss, and that fellow, Guy Topock, that was Cooper's pardner. They've been stealing our cattle and pulling all these raids—Oh, I've heard plenty since

236

I've been here. I—I think they intended to kill me."

But Smith was no longer listening; he was staring hard at Cooper. "What you got to say to that?"

"I wouldn't waste my breath," Cooper snarled, "tryin' to—"

"It would *be* a waste of breath," Jane agreed, "because—"

"Well I think I'll take the both of you in," Smith scowled at Bufe and Cooper. "Telldane's wanted for the murder of Brill and—"

"But he didn't murder Brill—he hasn't murdered *anyone*," Jane flashed. "Andy Cooper murdered Brill; killed him for his money belt—he told me so himself—thought it was a great joke that you were fixed to pin it on Bufe. And Guy Topock robbed the stage—"

"You certainly know all the answers," Smith scowled.

"Of course! Don't you *understand?* Gus Pring intended to—to murder me—they didn't care how they talked. Why, Vargas discovered gold on Father's land—an old mine or something that's been closed for years. He was going to double-cross Gus, but Gus found out about it."

"I guess you better unlimber some talk," Deef Smith told Cooper grimly. And finally, sullenly, Cooper did, confirming Jane's declarations. He must have realized there was no way out; and

237

a little later, handcuffed, Smith took him off to town.

And when they were gone, Bufe said to Jane: "Words ain't much use at a time like this. I reckon I owe you—"

"Nonsense! You owe me nothing—the owing is all on my side. Father told me how you came out here because he asked you to—of all you've been doing to help him. Poor Dad. It hurt him pretty bad to find how Gus had taken him in—I guess Gus took about everyone in. I—" She broke off and Bufe saw tears in her eyes; knew she was thinking of her father.

He stood there, twisting his hat, trying to think of something to say. But words seemed puny things to console the loss of a father. What he finally did say was, "I—Well—I guess I better be shovin' on. Things'll be quietin' down round here; won't be much work for a gun fighter. Expect I'll drift on over the hump . . . I— uh—Jane, I'm mighty sorry I've been such a fool—such a miserable—"

"Shh!" Jane wiped a sleeve across her cheeks. "You've—"

"No. I been a fool. No faith nor charity nor anything else. Just a gun fighter, an' I guess that's all I ever *will* be. I—I want you to know I realize it; that I'm sorry for the things I've thought of you an' called you—that I ain't blamin' you at all for throwin' me over. I—Well, goodbye—"

"You—you're not really leaving?"

Bufe nodded. He smiled sourly. "I expect things'll quiet down better if I'm off someplace else—things usually do, I've noticed."

"But—but I've been kind of hoping you'd take over the Flying K and—"

"Nope—'Fraid not." The prospect of being around where he would see her every day, where he could realize more keenly—if that were possible—the things that might have been, held no allurement.

"But, Bufe—I *want* you to!"

He stared, amazed. His cheeks wrinkled up in puzzlement. "You—Say! I don't get this—"

"Don't—don't you care for me any more?"

"*Care* for you! Great grief! Why—But shucks; you can't mean—"

She nodded, smiling through her tears. "Of course. I've always loved you, Bufe—even when—when you acted so mannishly obstinate and mean, I—Oh! my dear!"

Center Point Large Print
600 Brooks Road / PO Box 1
Thorndike, ME 04986-0001 USA

(207) 568-3717

US & Canada:
1 800 929-9108
www.centerpointlargeprint.com